Would he stop her?

He knew what she was up to.

Silently they measured each other from across the room. The dull pounding of her heart was like a distant echo in Samantha's ears. Vaguely she wondered if Ross could hear it. His face was grim, his eyes intense. Unconsciously her gaze lingered on his mouth. Memories stirred, heating her. She had seen his mouth relaxed in laughter, sweet with tenderness, sensuous and possessive in passion. He could make her weak, make her ache. And after tonight she would never see him again. Except in her dreams. Somehow she knew he would always be in her dreams.

Dear Reader,

Spellbinder! That's what we're striving for. The editors at Silhouette are determined to capture your imagination and win your heart with every single book we publish. Each month, six Special Editions are chosen with *you* in mind.

Our authors are our inspiration. Writers such as Nora Roberts, Tracy Sinclair, Kathleen Eagle, Carole Halson and Linda Howard—to name but a few—are masters at creating endearing characters and heartrending love stories. Their characters are everyday people—just like you and me—whose lives have been touched by love, whose dreams and desires suddenly come true!

So find a cozy, quiet place to read, and create your own special moment with a Silhouette Special Edition.

Sincerely,

The Editors
SILHOUETTE BOOKS

LINDA TURNER
Shadows in the Night

Silhouette Special Edition

Published by Silhouette Books New York

America's Publisher of Contemporary Romance

SILHOUETTE BOOKS
300 East 42nd St., New York, N.Y. 10017

Copyright © 1986 by Linda Turner

ISBN: 0-373-09350-0

First Silhouette Books printing December 1986
Second printing January 1987

America's Publisher of Contemporary Romance

Printed in the U.S.A.

Books by Linda Turner

Silhouette Desire
A Glimpse of Heaven #220

Silhouette Special Edition
Shadows in the Night #350

LINDA TURNER

is not only a writer, but also a partner in a publishing company. She enjoys romance writing because it gives her a chance to travel extensively, and hopes to sail someday from Texas, where she makes her home, to Maine.

Prologue

A match flared in the darkness, briefly illuminating the man's rough, unrelenting features as he bent his dark head to light a cigarette. Shadows sculptured the contours of his face, carving out hollows under the hard angles of high cheekbones and clinging to the ragged growth of whiskers that darkened his determined jaw. His curly, almost black hair and the burnished copper of his skin spoke of Mexican ancestry somewhere in his family's past, yet his eyes were gray, glowing eerily in the meager light, missing little. As he shook out the match, the night swallowed him.

Under the cloak of darkness, he leaned against a parked car, apparently relaxed, his booted feet spread comfortably. But his nonchalance was only a guise. He was a suspicious man, at times a hard man, and he wasn't easily fooled. By anyone. At age thirty-six, life held few illusions for him. He had learned the hard way to protect his rear.

Down the road, the high whine of an engine raced through the night, but he didn't even look up. His eyes were trained on his companion, his face impassive, his thoughts cynical. He'd been a fool to think his resignation would be accepted without incident. During his years as a troubleshooter for the State Department, he'd only averted several dozen *minor* international incidents. Why should the government show him any gratitude for that? Crap! He'd taken his life in his hands too many times to remember, and now they were asking him to do it again. Just one more time. Like hell! They could just find someone else for the job.

His companion leaned against another car, his nerves tense, frustration eating away at his stomach like an ulcer. What was really going on behind that expressionless facade the younger man presented to the world? Mac wondered, his frown fierce. He no longer knew this man who had taken his grandmother's family name and now called himself Ross de la Garza, could barely recognize in him the rebellious adventure-seeking youth who had defied his father and joined the army to find the kind of life he didn't think he could find in West Texas. A life of danger and aliases, where there was no place for a past, a family. His need for the love and support of a family seemed to have died with his mother. Had Ross ever regretted the loneliness of the past eighteen years?

Mac was struck anew by the changes time and experience had wrought in the younger man, changes that had left him hard and mocking. He knew there was a soft side to Ross, a boyish side that occasionally peeked out from dancing eyes, but that side had been woefully absent this evening. More often than not, the light in the gray eyes was cynical rather than amused, and it was blatantly obvious that Ross was still dangerously attracted to the darker side of life. That, more than anything else, worried Mac. He frowned and threw down his own cigarette, grinding it out fiercely with the heel of his boot. What the hell was going on behind those cold gray eyes?

The smoke from Ross's cigarette floated like a ghost between Mac and him. He studied it for a minute before breaking the silence. "Okay, Mac, what's this all about? Why was I given orders to meet you in the middle of the desert? Why all the secrecy?"

"Because it wasn't safe to meet at the station," the older man admitted baldly. "What I have to say to you is confidential, and I couldn't take a chance that we'd be overheard or you'd be seen." When Ross made no comment, he sighed heavily. "West Texas has changed, Ross. When the Mexican government devalued the peso, illegal aliens started streaming across the border in droves, especially at Laredo and El Paso. We were pretty lucky around here—there are no large border towns nearby, and the only work available is on the ranches. So we kept a lid on it. Until recently." Bitterness laced his voice. "A smuggling ring called *Los Chisos* has set up an operation across the river in Ojenaga, and they've been shuffling aliens across the border like they're running a damn ferry. And I can't do a thing to stop them."

Ross frowned. "Why not?" he demanded. "Don't you have enough men?"

Mac laughed shortly, without humor. "I never have enough men. But that's not the problem. The smugglers know where we patrol and when. They know where traffic checks are set up. Everything. Someone at the station is tipping them off."

For a man with Terry MacArthur's pride, Ross knew this wasn't an easy admission to make. He studied him thoughtfully. "You don't have any clues as to who it is?"

"Do you think I'd have asked Washington for help if I knew who it was?" he snapped, frustration lighting the fuse on an already short temper. "It could be any one of my men—that's what's so frightening about it. I don't even know which one of them would be capable of such a thing. Last week an agent was almost kidnapped and two others just missed walking into an ambush." He glared at Ross as if he were the cause of his troubles. "Something's got to be done before someone gets hurt!"

The silence that followed his angry bellow was thick with tension. For one fleeting moment, defeat was bitter on Ross's tongue. They were asking a hell of a lot of him this time. His father's ranch was hardly a stone's throw from where they stood, and all his instincts urged him to forget the past, forget his damn pride, forget that his father told him to never come back. His old man was pushing seventy; it was time to end this bitterness between them and go home. But the government wanted him to catch the smugglers, instead. He swore softly. Let them find someone else.

But no one else would know the area as well as he. Even after all these years, he could still track a spider across the desert with his eyes closed, he thought wryly, without conceit. He was damn good, and he wasn't going to walk away from trouble this close to home. His eyes were clear, cool, assessing as they met Mac's. "You haven't got a snowball's chance in hell of breaking up the smuggling ring as long as you've got an informant in the office," he said bluntly. "You can't stop them on this side of the river as long as they know every move you're going to make before you make it."

"I hope you're not suggesting what I think you're suggesting," Mac growled.

White teeth flashed in the darkness. "You getting soft in your old age, Mac? You sound like an old woman."

"Damn it, man! I just want to make sure you know what you're getting into. What you're planning is against the law on both sides of the river. I won't be able to help you if you get caught in Mexico illegally."

Ross sobered. "Don't worry. I won't get caught. Once I infiltrate the ring I'll find out who the leaders are, and you can bust the whole gang. And your informant won't know a thing about me, so I'll be safe."

The older man's disapproval was almost tangible, but before he could veto the idea, Ross said quietly, "I know what I'm doing, Mac. Quit worrying. I've been in tighter spots than this. I can handle it."

He made no idle boast. He was the type of man who could handle practically anything. Thanks to his training in the army's special services unit, he had the instincts of a jungle cat and the well-honed skills of a guerrilla. After leaving the army, the government had called on his services, and for the past ten years, he had worked behind the scenes in innumerable hot spots around the world. He was an expert at trouble. A nameless face in the crowd, he was quick, thorough, successful. In any kind of a fight, only a fool would underestimate him.

"I know." Mac sighed heavily and crossed his arms over his chest. "But I don't have to like it. What about your resignation?"

Almost imperceptibly Ross's jaw tightened. Don't remind me, he thought in disgust. Once again he'd been outmaneuvered. But this was the last time. "Once you have your smugglers I'm through," he informed Mac. "I'm going to go back to the ranch and clear up some unfinished business. Then I'm going to sit on the porch and watch the traffic go by."

"What traffic?" Mac demanded. "You can't even see the road from your house."

"I know. I can't wait to get back to it. I've missed it."

At his simple admission, Mac sighed in relief. The boy wasn't as far gone as he'd thought. "Aren't you afraid you might be recognized around here?"

"No. I haven't been home in eighteen years, Mac, and I was just a kid when I left. I've become pretty good at disguises, too. With long hair and a beard, even my old man would mistake me for an out-of-luck drifter who'd do just about anything for money.'' He straightened away from the car, suddenly anxious to get on with the job at hand. ''Nothing must change at the station, or the informant will be suspicious. So don't worry when you don't hear from me. I probably won't show up until I've got all the information you need.''

Mac withered him with a glance. ''Of course I'll worry,'' he snapped. ''Once you're across the river, you're going to be totally on your own. Don't take any more risks than you have to.''

Gray eyes glinted in the darkness, a black brow lifted innocently. *''Moi?''*

Mac snorted, not fooled in the least. ''You're damn right. You always were a daredevil.''

Ross chuckled, his grin wicked. ''I still am, Mac. I still am.''

Chapter One

The hunter and the hunted stalked the desert floor, the whispered sounds of the chase desperate in the night. Samantha Spencer lifted her binoculars and once again tried to pierce the blackness that shrouded the secret crevices of the riverbank, ignoring the struggles for survival that went on around her. Sheer limestone cliffs towered in the distance, intimidating, silent, magnificent. The Big Bend country of Texas was trapped in time, the Rio Grande somehow escaping the civilizing touch of man, its mysterious and often treacherous currents sliding in and out of stark canyons and hidden coves that even today offered shelter to those running from the law. Under the concealing cloak of darkness, shadows moved in the night. It was all too easy to let the imagination have free rein and to mistake the gentle lapping of the river against its banks for the splash of an oar. It was a sinister night, the kind that encouraged men to shoot first and save the questions for later. Samantha hoped to God no one was trigger-happy.

A cool wind rippled across the river to tease the auburn curls that had escaped the thick plait hanging down her back to her waist. Her one claim to vanity, she thought wryly. It would have been so much more practical to cut it, but she could carry practicality only so far. As a teenager, she had struggled to arrange the fiery strands that seemed to have a life of their own, at times even cursed her fate, but as a woman she knew her hair was her best feature. The wild red curls added fullness to her thin face and hopefully downplayed the thousands of freckles she had learned to live with. By no stretch of the imagination could she be called beautiful—she was too thin, her mouth too large—but intelligence lit her deep-blue eyes. And she'd rather have brains than beauty any day. Although her chin was too rounded for her taste, there was a strength of character there. Her confidence seldom wavered.

A shiver raced down her spine and she silently zipped up her bottle-green jacket. The days were already hinting at the summer heat to come, but the March nights were still chilly and long. Thank God this one was almost over.

The reeds along the riverbank rustled. Samantha's cobalt-blue eyes swung to her partner, L. J. Reynolds, who sat tensely at her side, before she whirled, her hand automatically reaching for the gun at her hip.

She froze, her breath trapped in her lungs as she listened for the slightest whisper of movement. Nothing. Perhaps it was an animal in search of a drink, or a snake. With a sigh, she relaxed and settled against the rock she had been using as a backrest, the utter silence that surrounded them easing the accelerated beat of her heart into a steady, reassuring cadence. "Another false alarm," she whispered as L.J. echoed her sigh.

"The whole night's been a false alarm," he grumbled irritably, making no attempt to lower his voice. "It's almost dawn, Sam. Don't you think it's time you admitted defeat?"

"No! I know this is it, L.J. It has to be!"

Her searching eyes scanned the Mexican side of the river, frustration tightening the angular line of her jaw. She'd been so sure this was the spot where the smugglers were ferrying illegal aliens into the U.S. Located right on the edge of Big Bend National Park, it was isolated and over seventy miles from the nearest border patrol station in Presidio. There were no electronic cameras in this remote area, no watchful eyes to note the illegal entry of a *coyote*, a Mexican smuggler, with his human cargo. The park was vast, with many of its acres empty and providing ample hiding places. Under the cover of darkness, it would be easy for the Mexican nationals to slip through the deserted countryside and make their way to work on nearby ranches, or go on to El Paso, where they could disappear in the barrios.

Anger gnawed at Samantha, chewing at the self-control she seldom let slip. Damn the *coyotes* for the yellow cowards that they were! And the group she and L.J. were after was the worst of the lot. *Los Chisos*. The ghosts. How she despised them. They were men without conscience, ruthless outlaws who transported the poor and desperate across the river for an outrageous fee, only to leave them ill-equipped for the desert they must cross to reach civilization. Like the wraiths they'd named themselves after, they slipped under the nose of the border patrol, just out of reach, leaving only their tracks behind as a mocking reminder of their passage. It was a vicious game they played, and they always seemed to win.

They had to be crossing here. It was the only logical place. This was one of the few breaks in the canyons that guarded the riverbank for miles in either direction. All her gut instincts, all the tracks, had led her to this spot. She couldn't be wrong, not after she'd had to talk long and fast to convince Mac to at least give her a chance to prove her theory.

"You're crazy!" Terry MacArthur, the patrol agent in charge of the Presidio office, had growled in a gravelly voice when she had requested the assignment during a meeting with several agents in his office. Years of working in the sun had carved the blunt features of his face in bronze and washed out the dark strands of his thick hair. He was a big man, still solid as a rock at fifty, and when he growled, the men under him backed off warily. He'd never married because, Samantha suspected, he'd never found a woman who could see past the gruff exterior to the twinkle in his eyes. She had noticed it immediately, even though he hadn't exactly welcomed her with open arms when she had been assigned to the Presidio office two months ago. He didn't approve of women in the field, and everyone knew it, including the higher-ups in Washington. But if he had expected Samantha to be intimidated by his blustering disapproval, he was sadly mistaken. She had met it head-on, and in their constant squabbling, they had developed a healthy respect for each other.

"I know I'm right about this, Mac."

"This isn't San Diego," David Martínez had cut in with a patronizing smile as he leaned back in his chair and crossed his arms over his broad chest. "We don't have the manpower they have out there, or the equipment."

A fifteen-year veteran who knew the Rio Grande like the back of his hand, David took great delight in reminding Samantha that she was a newcomer and, despite her two years' experience in California, still considered a novice. She had smiled sweetly at him, unperturbed. *He* wasn't the one she had to convince. "That's why we can't afford to overlook anything, David. Sometimes it pays to follow up a hunch."

Mac snorted. "The desert is dangerous, and it's no place for a female to be wandering around by herself. Especially at night."

Samantha flashed him a teasing grin. "Watch it, Mac," she warned. "You're beginning to sound like a chauvinist."

"You're damn right," he snapped. "The border patrol's no place for a lady."

"I'm not a lady. Ask my mother. She's been telling me that for years."

"One of these days, Spencer, that smart mouth of yours is going to get you into trouble," he warned. "All right, so you're not a lady. You're a female, aren't you?"

Samantha lifted her chin, undaunted. She'd had to prove herself before, despite her training and experience, and she'd come to accept the fact that men invariably got hung up on appearance. Dressed in her dull green uniform, with her braid hanging down her back like a teenager, she knew she looked deceptively slim and frail. There had been a time when her mother had despaired of ever getting her out of the trees in her backyard and into a dress. She was small—skinny, in fact—but she was also as tough as an old boot. There was no need to treat her like spun glass.

"Come on, Sam," Greg Saunders teased affectionately, "don't try to deny it. A man would have to be blind not to see how well you fill out your uniform." Tall, dark and handsome, with laughing blue eyes and a ready smile, Greg was a known flirt. "You're gorgeous, sweetheart."

The grimness on Mac's brow only deepened at the sound of the men's laughter. "If I let you go through with this," he told her sternly, "you're going to find yourself sixty miles from the nearest backup. You know how desperate some of these people are. They're not going to pay any attention to a five-foot-two slip of a girl who must weigh all of a hundred pounds dripping wet. What are you going to do if they don't cooperate? Shoot them?"

"Five foot four," she corrected him inconsequentially. Didn't he know by now that she was more than capable of taking care of herself? Her eyes reproached him. "I can shoot better than any man on the force, including you. If I have to, I can chase down a runaway and wrestle him until I get him handcuffed. I have yet to lose a 'wet,' but that doesn't seem to matter. I'm one of your best agents, and all you ever assign me to is traffic check."

She leaned over and flicked disdainfully at the rap sheets littering the top of his desk, her eyes lingering on the black-and-white photos attached to the records. "Ross de la Garza, Manuel Cortéz, Raúl Sandoval," she read. "You've already told us these men are suspected members of *Los Chisos*. They're getting away with murder, and you need every agent you've got. My God, Mac, what are you saving me for?"

"How about marriage and motherhood," he suggested in a voice as dry as West Texas. Not one of them recognized Ross from the picture he had deliberately circulated in order to increase the agent's credibility as a member of the smuggling ring, Mac thought in relief. Ross had passed the first test. Mac frowned at Samantha in irritation. "There's more to life than the border patrol. Why don't you find yourself a nice guy and get married?"

"Are you volunteering for the job?" she asked sweetly, grinning broadly.

"Aw, Sam, you don't want to get married," Greg protested in mock horror before Mac could open his mouth. "Do you know how many single women there are in Presidio? You can't deplete the ranks."

"She wouldn't go out with you, anyway," L.J. said cuttingly. "Not if she wants to have a good time. You're only interested in one thing..."

"You two should thank your lucky stars I'm married," David quipped, his brown eyes laughing as he watched them squabble. "Sam wouldn't look twice at either one of you if I were free."

"Sorry to disappoint you gentlemen," Samantha replied airily as her dancing eyes lingered on her boss. "But didn't I ever tell you I prefer older men?"

Mac scowled at her, but the effect was totally ruined by the reluctant grin that pulled at his mouth. "Get out of here," he ordered with a chuckle. "You're a damn impertinent woman, Samantha Spencer, and I don't know what I ever did to deserve you."

"Whatever it was, it must have been wonderful."

"Out!"

"Okay, okay, I'm going," she said with a laugh as the others headed for the door and their respective assignments. From the safety of the doorway, she turned to confront Mac, her eyes sparkling with determination. "Are you going to let me check out that section of the river or not?"

"Hellfire and damnation, you're too stubborn for your own good!" He glared at her, the doubts that assailed him never reaching his eyes. If Samantha Spencer was the informant, he was a lousy judge of character and she was a damn good liar. He sighed in defeat. All he could do was give her the rope and pray she didn't hang herself. "All right. I'll give you tonight. But that's all. L.J. can go with you, and if you get into any kind of trouble, you radio in immediately. Understand?''

"Me!" L.J. gasped indignantly. "Damn it, chief, this is nothing but a wild-goose chase..." The words died on his tongue at Mac's stony glare, and he sighed in disgust. "Ah, hell, never mind."

Samantha tactfully ignored L.J. and shot the older man a grateful smile. "Thanks, Mac. You won't regret this."

"Women!" he muttered. "You've always got to have your own way. Well, you've got it. But if you come back empty-handed—which you will—I don't ever want to hear one of your harebrained ideas again. You got that?"

She grinned cheekily and winked. "Got it, Mac. But you're going to have to eat those words, you know."

How could she have been so cocky? she wondered morosely as her dark surroundings once again closed in, shutting out her memories. Only a fool would try to navigate this particular stretch of the river at night.

It would be a long time before she lived this down.

She should have known Mac was right. He was always right, except when he harped at her about the dangers of her job and the need to settle down with a husband. Did he realize how much he sounded like her mother and three older brothers?

She'd been cautioned about the wild streak of adventure that had run in her blood ever since she was old enough to climb her first tree. Her father had died when she was three, killed in the line of duty as an FBI agent. While she was too young at the time to remember him, his death had drastically affected the rest of her family. She'd grown up struggling against their overprotectiveness and the fear that she would follow in her father's footsteps. For years, they'd preached marriage and children to her, hoping she would finally settle down so they could quit worrying.

She snorted in disgust. She had come close to making that mistake once, and the memories of that turbulent relationship could chill her blood even now. Michael Burns had claimed he loved her, and for a while, she tried to convince herself that she was doing the right thing. But when Michael pressured her to give up her job in favor of a less dangerous one—a secretarial position—she'd realized she was taking the easy way out and doing what was expected of her rather than what she wanted. That type of life was fine for others, but she'd smother in it. Much to her family's horror, she'd broken the engagement and decided that she wasn't cut out for marriage. That was three years ago, and now at twenty-eight, she still found more excitement in the border patrol than she could in any man.

The sound of wood grating against rocks rent the quiet of the night, ripping into her musings. Samantha froze, listening, her breath catching in her throat. Was that a boat being pushed ashore? Her muscles coiled in readiness, her alert gaze swinging toward the sound, adrenaline racing her heart. Stealthily she reached for the high-powered flashlight that sat on the ground beside her, her eyes never leaving the rock-sheltered cove from which the sound had come. She felt L.J. stiffen beside her, but there was no time for reassurances, no time for planning what they would do next. They had only training and instinct to guide them.

The urge to rush the quarry almost pushed Samantha from her hiding place. Patience, she warned herself, as excitement bubbled through her veins. With infinite care, she stepped around a boulder and hid in its shadow, appalled at the sight that met her straining eyes. A small rowboat sat low in the shallow water near the riverbank, dangerously filled with passengers. Didn't they know what a chance they were taking? she thought in horror. The Rio Grande was infamous for its quicksand and whirlpools. If the boat had capsized in midstream, they could have all drowned.

"Andale! Andale!" Two men held the boat steady while a third urged the passengers to hurry as they splashed into the shallow water and waded ashore. Those who hesitated or stumbled were given a quick shove for their efforts.

Anger flashed in her blue eyes, and without stopping to think Samantha stepped forward, the high beam of her flashlight slicing through the night to stop the motley crew in their tracks. *"¡Esperen!"* she ordered hoarsely, daring anyone to disobey her command to hold up. *"¡No se muevan!"* Don't move. How easy it was to say the words, but this was one of the most critical parts of her job. She had only the authority in her voice to intimidate more than a dozen men bent on escape. She would use her gun only as a last resort.

Chapter Two

Damn!"

The angry curse ricocheted off the towering rocks of the cove, and for one precious moment, no one moved, no one hardly dared to breathe.

Samantha stood rooted to the ground, the foolishness of her impetuous command striking her full in the face as she realized L.J. had not followed her out from behind the rock. She faltered, her widened eyes trapped by the sight of a man who stood in the darkness, emitting an almost tangible fury. His face was all angles and planes, cast in shadows from which startling pale eyes glowed. The devil, Samantha thought dazedly. She'd come across the devil himself. There was a savage, untamed streak in him; she could see it in the arrogant tilt of his dark brows, the faintly mocking curve of a mouth that was incredibly sensuous. And his eyes! Trapped in the glaring beam of her flashlight, they were the color of the soft gray dawn, yet were also hard and cold, carrying a promise that heated her blood. She shivered, the echo of her own heartbeat pounding dully in her ears.

Ross de la Garza's nostrils flared at the scent of danger in the air; frustration knotted the tense muscles of a jaw darkened by the thick growth of his beard. From beneath fierce brows, his eyes narrowed to thin, wary slits, but he could see only a vague silhouette of the intruder who had so foolishly stepped into the cove. Suspicion tightened his gut. Had his identity somehow been discovered? He'd been careful to cover his tracks, and though he still hadn't a clue as to who the smugglers' leader was, he'd have sworn they had accepted him completely. So who the hell was on the other end of that flashlight? A border patrol agent?

His companions shifted their feet uneasily, their dark, ruthless eyes drawn to the shadowy recesses of the cove, and Ross felt his insides freeze. The intruder had to be an agent. But didn't he know he was staring death in the face? One impetuous border patrol agent posed no threat to these men. They were desperate, without scruples, and life held no great value for them. They would seek escape at any price.

Memories flashed, exploding in his mind, chilling him. Another night, another lifetime, he had unwittingly intruded on a similar scene. Only then his helplessness—he was unarmed—had forced him to watch from the shadows as innocent aliens were beaten and killed, the women raped. His own impotence had infuriated him, and it was a long time before he was able to forgive himself for that night.

But he was no longer eighteen, no longer an innocent. The ensuing eighteen years had taught him cunning, resourcefulness. Grim confidence thinned the sensuous curve of his mouth and turned his eyes steely. He was going to have to take the agent down—before his cover was blown, before another murder was committed. There was no other way.

Beneath faded jeans that molded the lean lines of his body, the sinewy muscles of his long legs tensed. No mistakes, he cautioned himself as he coolly measured the distance between the agent and himself. He had to put that light out, but one wrong move, one miscalculation, and it could all be over.

Permanently.

Without warning, he sprang.

And all hell broke loose.

One quick chop sent the flashlight spinning off into the darkness as Ross slammed into the unsuspecting agent and they both hit the ground hard. On the edge of his consciousness he heard the shouts of the smugglers as they scattered, but his attention was centered on the sheer terror that gripped the slim body he held pinned beneath him. Any type of reassurance was impossible.

From out of the darkness, an elbow flew at him and jabbed him in the ribs. He grunted in pain and grabbed at the arms and legs that suddenly struck him, cursing softly as his fingers closed around thin air. The man was as slippery as a snake! Ross lunged and threw himself across the wiry body, only to freeze as if he'd been kicked in the stomach. His stunned eyes locked on the heaving breast his hand covered before flying to the agent's face. A woman! Had Mac lost his mind?

An angry gasp tore at Samantha's lungs, searing her as surely as the hand that covered her breast. Instinct pushed aside the momentary panic that gripped her, and she fought wildly, lashing out at her assailant with a strength born of desperation. Her mind was clear and calculating as she kicked and aimed for the most vulnerable parts of her attacker's body—the eyes, nose, groin. The battle waged in a silence broken only by their labored breathing, and Samantha's frustrations mounted as he successfully fended off blow after blow. Somewhere in the back of her mind she knew she would lose—he was too big, too strong—but she'd be damned if she'd make it an easy victory for him!

With a twist of her wrist she was free. Her hand raced toward his face, his eyes. "Get your filthy hands off me!" she gritted through clenched teeth.

He stopped her hand just inches from his face, his fingers like talons around her slender wrist. Within seconds her arms were stretched above her head, her body trembling and vulnerable beneath that of a man who surely had to weigh three hundred pounds. She glared into piercing gray eyes and felt the blood drain from her face. The man in the shadows. The devil. The first faint stirrings of fear coiled in her stomach. There was no mercy in his eyes, no softness, just a grim determination that stabbed her in the heart. With a sickening lurch, she realized she didn't have a chance in hell of getting away from him.

Suddenly the earth seemed to give way beneath them, and Samantha screamed as the sandy riverbank crumbled and threw them both in the river. A shock of cold water hit her full in the face, choking her. In growing panic she reached for the devil who had knocked her down, sobbing in despair as her fingers grasped only water. The current swirled angrily around her, tossing her about like flotsam before swallowing her and dragging her down to its murky depths. Her feet slipped out from under her, and she couldn't get her footing in a world that was suddenly cold and dark. The need for air screamed through her. She struggled frantically, finally breaking through the surface with a strangled cry that was immediately snuffed out by another wall of water.

Ross jerked toward her, fear dropping into his stomach like a cement block as he saw her small body being buffeted about by the river. If she got pulled into the rapids, she wouldn't have the strength to get herself out. She had no business being out here!

He dove toward her just as the current swept her toward a huge boulder, his fingers clamping onto her dark red braid as it trailed behind her like a lifeline. With one quick tug, he pulled her free of the river's deathly hold and into his arms. Winded, he struggled with her to the bank and collapsed, bracing his arms on either side of her to keep from crushing her. Water ran in rivulets from his black hair, tracing the imperfections of his face, before dropping onto her pale countenance.

The silence that surrounded them was unnatural, deadly, broken only by their tortured breathing. A

chill of awareness slid down Ross's spine. He stiffened, abruptly lifting his head, his eyes alert. The riverbank was empty but for the two of them; the
rowboat listed, unattended, in the shallows. He
scanned the rocky shadows of the cove with sharp eyes
that pierced the pockets of darkness, but the ancient,
brooding cliffs only stared blankly back, refusing to
give up their secrets. He knew they were still out there;
he could feel them. The scent of danger was heavy in
the air, ominous, threatening. The smugglers were
waiting, watching his every move. If he wanted to keep
the trust he had so painstakingly built between them,
he had little choice but to do what was expected of
him. But he didn't like it. He didn't like it one damn
bit.

Samantha watched the grim emotions flicker across
his face and tried not to shiver as his gray eyes suddenly locked with hers. She struggled for breath, both
terrified and fascinated. Not an ounce of fat marred
the whipcord leanness of him, and even in the misty
light of dawn, she could see that his wet jeans and blue
work shirt were plastered to a body that was as tough
and rugged as the rock-strewn terrain. His face was,
like the desert, a study in contrasts. Thick, dark brows
and a nose that had obviously been broken gave him
a look of hardness, yet the fierce glare of the sun had
etched laugh lines at the corners of his eyes and baked
his skin to a deep, golden bronze. Water glistened in
his long scraggly black hair, and the ragged beard that
shadowed his rock-hard jaw gave him the ruthless look
of a desperado. Samantha tried not to cringe as his
steely gray eyes returned her perusal from just inches

away, the smile playing about his sensuous mouth more than a little threatening. He was weathered, ageless, dangerous. But there was something about him...

She searched his face, frowning at the elusive memory that nagged her. His mouth, those eyes—where had she seen them before? There was something so familiar there. Suddenly recognition slapped her in the face and she gasped, her blue eyes large pools of shock in her pale face. His picture! She had seen it on Mac's desk. Along with two other members of *Los Chisos*. The blood drained from her face in a rush. He wouldn't think twice about killing her.

Ross watched the recognition, the suspicion, dawn on her face and cursed hotly. Just how the hell did she know him? He'd never laid eyes on her before; he was sure of it. But she knew him, damn it. Icy anger gripped him. He could see the words trembling on her lips, the accusations, and any minute her wagging tongue was going to destroy everything. They'd never get out of the cove alive. "Don't say it," he warned threateningly.

"I know you," she whispered hoarsely, ignoring his order. "You're—"

One carefully aimed blow to the jaw knocked her cold. Ross watched her go limp, his lips thinning as regret stole over him. Her jaw would be tender when she regained consciousness, but she'd left him no choice. Was she the informant? Even if she was, how would she know him? Only Mac knew of his presence in West Texas. Damn! If he was sure she was the informant, she deserved much more than a cold sock to the jaw. But there was also a possibility that dumb luck had led her to this particular spot at the exact time they were crossing. For some reason he couldn't fathom, he wanted to give her the benefit of the doubt, even though he didn't believe in luck. God, he was getting too old for this!

The sight of her still figure wrenched at his gut, and without conscious volition, he smoothed the wet strands of hair back from her pale face. He wasn't in the habit of hitting women. He laughed suddenly, wryly. She might be a woman, but right now, she looked like a drowned rat.

Her hair was a tangled mess, but even wet, it seemed to have a life of its own. Ross reached out to touch the burnished copper strands and stopped, his face grim. She looked so small, so fragile. Protectiveness surged in him, catching him off guard, and he jumped to his feet, scowling. What the devil was wrong with him? Fragile, hell! He'd never met a woman who needed less protection. She was bold, brassy, and strong as a horse, even if she was ten pounds underweight. But her hair was the stuff dreams were made of! Images flashed before him, taunting him. He could see her naked, her hair swirling about her slim hips, beckoning him. Those fiery curls could tempt a man to wickedness.

Ross cursed softly as his body stirred with unexpected desire. Forget her, de la Garza, he cautioned himself sternly. She's a wildcat, and she's already come damn close to destroying months of work. Without a backward glance, he turned toward the hidden crevices of the cove.

"Muy bueno, amigo," Manuel Cortéz mockingly applauded as he stepped out from behind a concealing rock and strode toward him. "But you should have let her drown. It would have saved us the trouble of killing her." Small, wiry, with a touch of cruelty in his brown eyes, Manuel Cortéz ran the smuggling operation from the Mexican side of the river with a ruthlessness that few men could equal. He wouldn't hesitate to kill if he felt threatened.

Ross's gray eyes glinted like the sharp, deadly blade of a knife. The girl's life, his own, hinged on how well he handled the next few minutes.

"She's an agent," Ross told him flatly. "You kill her, and you're going to have every border patrol agent between Brownsville and San Diego breathing down your neck."

"She's seen us, *amigo*."

"So has her partner." Raúl Sandoval, the other smuggler, stepped into the clearing holding a gun on a tall, blond agent. "We have no choice but to kill them."

"You do, and the U.S. government will hunt you down like the miserable snakes that you are," L.J. ground out hoarsely.

"Shut up!" Raúl snarled, nudging the agent forward with the gun. "Do you think anyone can find us once we slip back across the river? Don't kid yourself, my friend."

"Take care of him," Manuel ordered. "I'll kill the woman, and then let's get out of here. We're going to miss the pickup if we don't hurry."

"And *El Chiso*? What will you tell him?" Ross demanded silkily. "You said our orders were only to harass the agents, not kill them."

Manuel's black eyes narrowed to suspicious slits. "Is there some reason you don't want to kill them?"

Ross shrugged indifferently, his face impassive. "I can think of other uses for a woman than killing her, but don't let me stand in your way. You're the one who answers to *El Chiso*." Ross watched the doubts flicker across Raúl's face, and pressed his advantage. "Why not take them captive? Let *El Chiso* decide if they should live or not."

"And who will take them back to the cabin?" Manuel demanded.

Ross's cool gaze met his unflinchingly. "Why you, of course. Raúl and I will make our delivery and meet you back there."

Manuel laughed softly, mockingly. "You are very clever, *amigo*. But this time I think I will make the delivery. Raúl can take the boat back and then the two of you can take our friends here to the cabin. ¿*Sí*?"

Ross shrugged. "Whatever you say." Without the least bit of effort, he lifted the unconscious woman and slung her over his shoulder. "Let's go, Raúl."

The sun burned red-hot against the top of Samantha's head, playing with the fiery strands of her hair. Her eyelids flickered against her pale cheeks, the blackness that shrouded her mind lifting jerkily, reluctantly, until she gradually became aware of the sizzling caress of the sun. She winced, her eyes squinted tightly closed, and tried to turn away from the heat, but dusty, coarse hair rubbed like a bristle brush against her cheek, and there was no escape. With a groan, she forced her eyes open.

And found her nose only inches from a blue-jean-clad knee.

She frowned, her confusion abruptly turning to shock as she suddenly noticed the uncomfortable sway of her body and the growing numbness of her hands and feet. I'm on a horse, she thought in dismay, her stomach jarring with each plodding step the animal took as it made its way across the rough desert terrain. With her feet hanging over one side of its neck and her arms over the other, she was slung across its back like so much excess baggage!

"Well, well, I see Sleeping Beauty awakes. Enjoying the ride?"

Samantha stiffened. That voice—she knew that voice! The grogginess that still muddled her brain suddenly vanished. With a gasp of pure outrage, she remembered the smugglers, the scuffle in the dark, her near drowning, and Ross de la Garza. Dear Lord, he had knocked her out! And now he was kidnapping her! Despite her ignoble position, she jerked her head up off the horse's neck and turned to glare at the man who sat only inches away with an infuriating grin on his bearded face. "You...scum! Just what do you think you're doing?"

His grin was quick, mocking, wicked. "I thought I was giving you a ride."

His smile almost rocked her heart from its mooring, horrifying her. Had she lost her mind? The man was a criminal! She glared at him as if he had just crawled out from under a rock. "Is that what you're going to tell the FBI when you're arrested for kidnapping?" she taunted. "You were just giving me a ride?"

Ross laughed and sent her sliding to the ground with a flick of his wrist. "Look around, lady. I know one side of the Rio Grande looks just like the other, but as far as you're concerned, this is the wrong side. In other words, sweetheart, the cavalry ain't comin'."

"They're going to kill us, Sam. They're just waiting for orders from *El Chiso*."

Samantha whirled, an icy wave of fear driving the blood from her face until her freckles stood out in bold relief. L.J. stood only a few feet away. Dusty, bruised, disheveled, he was a far cry from the neat California blonde she'd occasionally dated during the past two months. He was scared; she could see it in his eyes.

Samantha shot Ross a look that could have killed at fifty paces and hurried to the other man's side. "L.J., are you all right? What happened?"

"Did you hear me?" he cried hoarsely. "They're going to kill us! And it's all your fault! Why in the name of God did you step out from behind that rock?"

Samantha's concern quickly turned to anger. "In case you've forgotten," she replied icily, "it's our job to arrest these creeps. If you'd have stood beside me instead of hiding, we wouldn't be in this mess."

"Now, now, children," Ross mocked, "don't fight. There'll be time for that later, and we've got a long way to go before dark. Get moving."

Only a fool would fail to recognize this as an order, and despite L.J.'s criticism, Samantha was no fool. But she wouldn't go meekly to her own execution, either.

"Don't do anything stupid," L.J. hissed, easily spotting the stubborn set of her jaw. He grabbed her arm and pulled her along beside him as Ross trailed behind them on his horse. "Even if you could get away, we're in the middle of the desert, miles from the river. You'd never make it."

"We can't be that far from the river," she argued quietly. "I wasn't out that long."

"It doesn't take long to put you in a van and cart you into the interior. We're at least thirty miles from the border."

"I don't care if we're a hundred. They're going to kill us, anyway. If I see an opening, I'm going to make a run for it. If you've got any sense—which I'm beginning to doubt—you will, too."

"Shut up and walk!" Ross growled, urging his horse closer. "It won't do you any good to plot an escape. I'd catch you before you took three steps."

Samantha bit back an angry retort and tried to keep up with L.J., but every step was an exercise in torture. Her jacket made her feel as if she were trapped in a sauna, and with a mumbled oath she peeled it off, only to wince in pain as it fell from her fingers to the sandy ground. Her blouse was as rough as wet sandpaper on her tender skin, sticking to her shoulder blades, the grit from the river rubbing her raw. And her cheeks were already starting to sting from the direct rays of the sun and the abrasive whip of the wind.

What condition would she be in after spending the hottest part of the day in the direct sunlight?

She had to escape! she thought frantically as her eyes wildly searched her surroundings. The hot sun beat down on the desert floor, baking the earth to a dull, parched brown. There wasn't a sign of humanity or water for miles in any direction. The terrain was stark, empty, dry. Only the wild and untamed belonged there, only those with something to hide could appreciate its barrenness. She shivered, her blue eyes hard. Her only consolation was that Ross de la Garza was out here in this emptiness and heat, too, and she hoped he fried!

The sun dragged its way across the clear sky at a snail's pace, and even though they'd been traveling only a little over an hour, Ross called several rest breaks. His cool gray eyes narrowed against the sun's glare, he watched Samantha push herself to keep up with her partner, her gaze surreptitiously scouting her surroundings. His jaw tightened, thinning his mouth into a hard, impatient line. She was going to cause more trouble than she was worth; he could feel it in his bones. He'd seen the fear in her eyes when she'd realized the hopelessness of her situation. With any other woman, that would have been enough to assure him that she'd be cowed into following orders until he could figure out a way to get her out of this mess. But not with Red. He'd have had to be blind to miss the spark of rebellion in her blue eyes or the defiant lift of her chin. She'd go bear hunting with a switch, and that was what worried him. He hoped to God she'd take her partner's advice and not do anything stupid.

Sudden mischief sparkled in Ross's eyes and pulled his mouth into a reluctant grin. Damn, but she had a short fuse. If looks could kill, he'd have dropped dead when she regained consciousness. He hadn't been able to stop himself from goading her. She really would want to murder him when she found out that he was on the same side of the law she was!

If she lived that long.

He sobered at the thought, anger rippling along his jaw. Did Red have any idea how lousy her timing was? Right now, he had enough information to shut down the operation on the Mexican side of the river. But that wasn't good enough. Someone else would just set up another operation under the very nose of the *Federales*, the Mexican federal undercover police, and with the right kind of persuasion, the Mexican officials would conveniently look the other way. He cursed to himself tersely. Wasn't the same thing happening on the American side of the river?

Icy fury invaded his eyes. Who the hell was the weak link in the border patrol? Whoever he was, he was a cool customer and a son of a bitch. Only a monster could report to work each day, gain the trust of his fellow workers and then send them into an ambush and possible death. He was cold, scheming, diabolical—and probably the last person anyone would ever suspect. Suddenly the memory of stormy sapphire eyes dark with anger and small fists pounding his body teased him. Ross winced, rubbing his chest, his eyes thoughtful as they rested on Samantha. Was she capable of that type of subterfuge? No. Her actions had been based on honest anger, not deceit. And she had too much fire in her blood to be that cold and ruth-less.

The relief that coursed through him irritated the hell out of him, and he angrily spurred his horse to a faster pace, crowding his prisoners until they quickened their strides. He was acting like a fool. He knew the dangers of letting a woman get under his skin when he was on an assignment; he'd always sworn he'd never be that stupid. And he hadn't. Wisps of memory drifted across his mind like a distant fog, dragging up the past. The sloe-eyed beauty in Afghanistan, the long-legged temptress in the South American jungle, the cool sophisticated blonde in Washington—not a one of them had touched his concentration. He had walked away without a second look, a second thought. And he was damn sure going to do it again. Red was nothing but a scrawny package of trouble, and if the opportunity ever presented itself, he'd take her. Maybe then the reality would drive away the thought of how she'd feel under him.

The heat in his loins mocked his resolve, and a self-derisive smile curled his lips. Who was he trying to fool? His present concentration was nonexistent. His superior would never believe it. Hell, he didn't believe it. He should have never let Mac talk him into this, and if the assignment had been anywhere but in West Texas, he would have turned him down flat. For years he'd been living on the edge—the edge of the law, the edge of death—and he'd had his fill of surviving by his wits. It was a lonely life, filled with empty nights and lies, distrust and danger. Maybe he was burned out, or just getting old, but the dream of returning to the quiet life of the ranch appealed to him more and more. Once he came out of the shadows, he'd never go back.

He'd made countless runs with the smugglers over the past two months. Eight weeks of hiding in the dark, running for the river, running for his life. By now he knew the procedure by heart.

Manuel and Raúl made nightly trips into Ojenaga, their experienced eyes quickly noting the desperation that clouded the faces of the poor and out of work who were contemplating the crossing to *el norte*. It took little persuasion to convince them to return with the smugglers to the ramshackle house high in the mountains outside of Ojenaga where they waited for a sign from their guides that it was their time to cross. Sometimes they waited for several hours, sometimes a week, in roach-infested quarters that weren't fit for a dog.

When the decision was made to move, not a second was wasted. The aliens were herded down the mountain to where the battered van was concealed, then loaded up like sheep and driven out into the barren countryside. The driver of the van left them in a deserted spot, and it was Ross and Raúl's job to lead the group to the river, where they always found Manuel waiting with the rowboat. The actual crossing was the easy part. Up until last night, they had penetrated the border without incident.

Ross's hands tightened on the reins, his mouth grim. Someone was making those calls to the smugglers, keeping them posted on the nightly whereabouts of the border patrol and telling them where to land. How much did Red know? Could he trust her?

He couldn't trust anyone, he reminded himself bitterly. Appearances were deceptive, and until he broke this ring open, he'd keep his own counsel, just as he always had. For all their sakes, it was imperative that his two prisoners think he was exactly what he appeared—a greedy bastard who'd do just about anything for money. He'd already taken one chance by stopping Manuel from killing her and her partner, and he couldn't afford to take another.

Not when he was so close to *El Chiso* he could almost smell him.

Once every week, their pockets bulging with the money they had taken from the aliens, Manuel and Raúl disappeared into the desert before Ross could follow them. He wouldn't let that happen again. The next time there was a meeting with *El Chiso*, he was damn sure going to be there.

They reached the foothills an hour later, and Samantha knew it was only a matter of time before she collapsed. How far had they come? she wondered wearily. Five miles? Ten? She ached in every bone in her body, the slightest breeze burned her scalded skin and her lack of sleep the previous night had left her decidedly light-headed. Why was she driving herself this way, allowing Ross de la Garza to herd her to her death? If he was going to kill her, he could do it here. She wasn't taking another step.

"No more," she said hoarsely, her throat as dry as the wind that whipped her hair about her sunburned face. "I'm not going any farther."

"Sam, don't be a fool!" L.J. cried, staring at her as if she'd lost her mind. "He'd just as soon shoot you as look at you."

Samantha's eyes locked with those of her captor. "No, he won't. Not until he gets the okay from *El Chiso*."

Ross grinned, reluctant admiration shining in the depths of his eyes. He had to give her credit; she didn't lack for guts. "I may not kill you right now," he retorted, "but there's nothing to stop me from roping you and dragging you behind my horse. Walk or be dragged. The choice is yours."

"You wouldn't!" she gasped, outraged.

"Try me, sweetheart."

His quiet growl slid around her like an icy north wind, chilling her to the bone. He meant it. She could see it in the ruthless set of his dark, bearded jaw, the almost feral gleam in his eyes. He wouldn't tolerate any opposition.

"Eh, *amigo*, what's this?" Raúl teased as he came around the curve of a hill toward them. "Is that any way to charm the *señorita*? She'll think we're all heartless."

"But we are," Ross retorted with a grin. "What took you so long? And where's your horse?"

The Mexican cursed in disgust. "He stepped in a rabbit hole about a mile back. Worthless animal! We need a jeep."

Ross grinned, completely unsympathetic. The cabin was chosen as their hideout because of its inaccessibility. The string of horses that were kept at the foot of the mountains with the van was the only method of transportation other than by foot. "Not even a jeep could make it over these rocks. How about a drink before we get started again?"

L.J. watched Ross edge his horse up to where the smuggler stood. When he leaned over to hand him the canteen, L.J. gave Samantha a shove. "Run, Sam! Now!"

For a frozen moment, Samantha was too stunned to move, but at the sight of L.J. running as if his life depended on it, adrenaline pumped into her veins, and her feet barely touched the ground as she took off in the opposite direction. She knew from experience there was a lot more to the desert than cactus and creosote bushes. A network of arroyos crisscrossed the land, breaking the deceptive flatness of the plain with their deep crevices. During the rainy season, the arroyos could become raging torrents within a matter of minutes. And during a dry spell, they could hide an army. If she could only reach one . . .

The pounding of a horse's hooves thundered in the quiet of her desolate surroundings, echoing her labored breathing. Samantha went cold, then hot, a sudden flash of fear sickening her. Ross de la Garza. She had known he would come after her, but she hadn't expected him to close in on her this fast. She needed more time!

Panting, her eyes wild, she looked over her shoulder and found herself snared by the hard, merciless lines of his face, the icy depths of his eyes. She blanched. What would he do when he caught her?

The answers her imagination supplied terrified her, and without a thought she plunged down into the arroyo she had so desperately been seeking. The loose dirt gave beneath her weight and she half stumbled, then quickly righted herself as she ran, away from him, away from her fears.

Ross saw the terror on her face and swore softly as he urged his horse down into the arroyo after her. Damn it, if Raúl saw her escaping across the desert, he wouldn't hesitate to put a bullet through her. He jerked at the coiled rope tied to his saddle.

The lasso whistled over her head before settling around her shoulders, and Samantha cried out in surprise as her frantic escape was brought to an abrupt halt. She yanked at the rope, but it only tightened warningly, biting into the tender skin of her arms. Stay calm, she ordered herself sternly. But it was hard to think rationally when she turned to find him grinning at her with that mocking smirk on his face. If she ever got free, she'd make him wish he'd never been born!

"You might as well let me go," she said tightly. "You're never going to get away with this."

"Not on your life, lady," he said, chuckling, automatically backing the mare when Samantha stepped toward him. "You've been nothing but trouble from the beginning. Maybe it's time I showed you just who's in charge around here." Laughter danced in his eyes as he dismounted and slowly came toward her, making sure to keep the rope taut with each step. "Raúl's probably taken care of your partner by now, so it's just you, me and the snakes. This will be a lot more pleasant for both of us if you'll just cooperate."

"I'm not interested in making things pleasant for you," she retorted contemptuously, her sapphire eyes snapping. "And *when* I get free of you, Mr. de la Garza, I'm going to do everything in my power to see that you rot in jail."

He grinned and tugged her toward him. "Care to take bets on that?"

Samantha's gaze narrowed dangerously, her alert gaze noting his laughter, his relaxed hold on the rope as he slowly eliminated the distance between them. One of the first lessons she'd learned in self-defense was the value of surprise. Without warning, she launched herself at him.

Too late, Ross tried to ward her off, but she butted him in the chest with her shoulder, sending them both to the ground in a tumble of arms and legs. A fist pounded his midriff with surprising strength, and he grunted in pain, irritation quickly sizzling into anger. "You little wildcat!" he thundered. "You're asking for it." He wrapped his arms around the small fury she presented and rolled over until he could straddle her. He'd only take so much abuse from a woman, and if she wanted to play rough, he'd be happy to oblige. He glared down at her, for the first time noticing her raw cheeks and sand encrusted hair. His anger melted. Every other woman he knew would have dissolved in tears if they'd found themselves in her situation. But not this skinny, hot-tempered woman. She was a fighter. And he liked her. Devilment burned in his eyes. "Are you going to behave yourself now?" he asked, grinning broadly.

"No!" Damn it, if only he weren't so quick, so strong! She'd almost had him.

He laughed softly. "Okay, have it your way, but you're only going to make it hard on yourself."

"I don't cooperate with smugglers." She twisted under him, clenching her teeth in frustration when he refused to budge. "You'd better think long and hard before you lay a hand on me, mister, because you're already looking at enough charges to put you away for a good long while. Smuggling, assault, illegal entry, kidnapping a federal agent . . ."

"Don't forget carrying a concealed weapon," he added with a chuckle, encouraging her misconceptions. As long as this little witch thought he was a *coyote*, he'd be relatively safe. "Lady, you're in a hell of a position to be making threats. I've got you at my mercy, and you know it."

His low, wicked laughter ran up her spine and raised sensitive hairs at the back of her neck. Samantha stiffened, suddenly achingly aware of the strength of his legs gripping her hips, of the power in his hard body, of the silence of the desert around them. He was so close she could see the roguish glint in his pale eyes and smell his masculine scent. She swallowed and prayed he couldn't feel her shaking body. How could she possibly reason with this man? He held all the cards. "Accosting me is only going to make things worse for you," she finally said coolly. "And don't think you'll get away with it. L.J. will get away, and when he gets back to the station, he'll call in the FBI."

"Your friend will be lucky to run a hundred yards before Raúl shoots him down," he stated flatly. "If he's your only hope, Red, then you haven't got a prayer."

His smugness irritated her. "*Someone* will come," she snapped. "But if you're going to rape me, hurry up and get it over with. I can't breathe."

For one deadly moment, she was terribly afraid he was going to accept her sarcastic offer. Again fear crawled into her stomach as her eyes scanned the unrelenting lines of his face. Had she lost her mind, goading this man that way? So far, he'd proved himself to be capable of anything.

Ross studied her thoroughly, his gaze lingering on her freckle-dusted cheeks, the sparkling anger in her incredibly blue eyes. What type of woman lurked beneath her prickly exterior? Didn't she know she wouldn't stand a chance against him or any other man who decided to take her? He suddenly pictured what might have happened to her if he hadn't been there when she confronted the smugglers, and his heart went cold. What the hell was Mac doing, letting her run around the desert? She was going to get her fool self killed if she wasn't careful.

Watch it, de la Garza, a mocking voice taunted him. You're getting soft. She's a luxury you can't afford. Look at her, for God's sake! She's a redheaded shrew, and she probably leads her men around by the nose. Is that what you want?

Ross scowled and rolled to his feet, reluctantly holding his hand out to her, his eyes cold. "No, thanks, I'll pass this time. C'mon, get up."

Samantha stared hard at his broad, callused hand. It was a strong hand, used to the rigors of hard work. There was strength and determination in his blunt fingers, with no sign of softness. How would that hand feel holding hers, touching the sensitive, hidden secrets of her body? Would he know how to be gentle?

Stunned by her thoughts, she looked up quickly at his face, and her heart stopped at the sight of his mocking grin. Her entire body flushed feverishly. She scrambled to her feet, ignoring his outstretched hand.

Ross stepped toward her and trapped her with his eyes. "Let me give you a little piece of advice, Red," he growled softly. "Don't try this fool stunt again if you want to live to see another sunrise."

Samantha lifted her chin. "Are you threatening me?" she demanded, forcing the words through a suddenly dry throat.

"You're damn right," he agreed, and abruptly jerked her into his arms. What did it take to intimidate this woman? "You've got no one to blame but yourself, you know. Hasn't anyone ever told you what kind of trouble big girls can get into in the dark?" he rasped thickly.

Samantha's heart slammed against her ribs. "No!"

He'd only meant to scare her, to put the fear of God in her for her own protection, but the minute he touched her, he knew it was a mistake. She was too close, too soft for rational thought. He swooped down to take her mouth, but at the touch of her surprised lips, need sprang quick and hot in his loins, stunning him. She wasn't supposed to taste like honey and feel like satin. The urge to bury himself in her softness threatened his control, and he groaned in despair. The timing was all wrong!

He released her so quickly, Samantha stumbled. Her eyes were wide with shock and her heart dropped crazily to her feet before shooting back up again. Where had he learned to kiss like that?

Ross reached out to gently close her mouth, his eyes alight with sudden laughter. He hadn't expected her to be speechless. "Close your mouth, sweetheart, or I'll think you want another."

Her jaw snapped shut, her eyes withering. "Don't flatter yourself. You're nothing but a common criminal . . ."

"Who can turn you on," he finished with a devilish grin. "Ain't life a bitch!" Laughing softly to himself at her livid expression, he walked back to his horse and mounted in one smooth motion that Samantha couldn't help but admire. Yet when he urged the animal toward her, she backed up warily.

"What are you doing? Trying to run me over to save yourself the trouble of shooting me?"

"So suspicious," he said ruefully, and held out his hand. "I'm only going to give you a ride. You look like you're about ready to drop, and we've got to catch up with Raúl and your friend."

"If Raúl didn't shoot him."

Ross's face turned grim. "There's always that possibility. He shouldn't have run. Come on, mount up." And before Samantha could argue further, he captured her wrist in an ironlike grip and hauled her up in front of him.

Samantha gasped. The unexpected heat of his thighs lying along the outside of hers melted her bones and turned her into a seething mass of awareness. Dear Lord, what was wrong with her? she wondered frantically. No man had ever affected her so strongly—so *instantly*! How could she feel this way about a man who was helping to plot her murder?

It's merely physical, she told herself sternly, and deliberately straightened her spine to avoid contact with Ross's hard chest. "I'd rather walk," she said icily, her eyes trained on the horse's flickering ears as he climbed out of the arroyo.

"So I can't touch you," Ross guessed with a chuckle that caressed her nape like a summer breeze. "Too bad. I happen to like touching you, and I'm calling the shots." With a devilish twinkle in his eyes, he gently touched the mare with his spurs, sending her into a gallop that threw Samantha back against him.

The curses that gathered on her tongue would have done a sailor proud, but she never had a chance to utter them. They came across Raúl almost immediately. Sitting on a huge boulder, his black eyes hard as he nursed a cut lip, he glared at Samantha. "Your friend—he got away. So what are we going to do with you, eh, *señorita*?"

Interlude

"What do you mean you don't know if she got away?" Mac thundered, outraged. "Didn't you wait to find out?"

Heat suffused L.J.'s sunburned face as he stood before Mac's desk like a schoolboy called before the principal. The other agents had gathered around him, their faces grim, accusing. Did they think he'd wanted to leave her? He'd argued with himself all the way back to the station about the wisdom of abandoning her, but he'd had no other choice. He couldn't rescue her alone. He needed help.

He drew himself up to his full height, despite the fact that he ached in every bone in his body. "If I'd have waited, I'd have been captured again," he defended himself stiffly. "That wouldn't have done either one of us any good."

Just the thought of Sam being in the hands of those cutthroats made Greg Saunders's blood run cold. "Do you think she got away?" he asked quietly.

"I don't know," L.J. replied wearily. He'd asked himself that same question countless times during the endless hours it had taken for him to make his way back across the river. "De la Garza went after her on a horse."

"Damn it, man, do you even know if she's alive or not?" Mac demanded in frustration.

L.J. met his piercing gaze unflinchingly. "No. But they won't do anything until they get a direct order from *El Chiso*. That's why they didn't kill us at the river."

An unfamiliar feeling of helplessness crawled into Mac's stomach as he studied the younger man. He had a bruise under his right eye, his uniform was torn and sweat stained, covered in a fine layer of dust, and he looked as though he were ready to drop where he stood. But appearances could be deceptive. For a man who had just escaped from a thieving group of murderers, L.J. was surprisingly short of information.

"If the smugglers had horses, how did you manage to escape?" Mac asked, not liking his suspicions but unable to ignore them. Was L.J. the informant? And if he was, what really happened in Mexico?

L.J.'s jaw clenched at the older man's tone. "Sandoval's horse went lame," he explained resentfully. "When Sam and I ran in opposite directions, he came after me while de la Garza went for Sam."

"Didn't he have a gun?" David Martínez demanded in surprise.

"Of course," L.J. snapped. "But I already told you they weren't going to kill us without a direct order from *El Chiso*! I hid behind a rock and jumped Sandoval from behind. I finally knocked him out and escaped in an arroyo. Luckily it was one that snaked off in a hundred different directions, and he wasn't able to track me when he came to."

The silence that fell over the office was thick with tension. All eyes turned to Mac. "What do we do now?" Greg Saunders asked. "We can't just leave her there."

"We wait," retorted Mac firmly.

"Damn it, Mac, that's Sam they've got! We can't just wait for them to kill her!"

"Don't you think I know that?" he growled bitterly. "But we can't rush off half-crazy into Mexico. Sam's resourceful. She may have escaped when L.J. did." With Ross's help, she might have. But he couldn't tell these men that, not when he still didn't know who the informant was. "It could take her hours, maybe even days, to find her way back across the river."

"And if she didn't escape?" David asked quietly.

"Then we'll hear soon enough," the older man replied heavily. "Once we know where she is, we'll plan our next course of action."

Chapter Three

The sun was low in the sky, casting long shadows on the desert floor, when Ross urged his horse up into the mountains. The rocky foothills gave way to steep inclines thick with juniper, pine and boulders, and the scorching heat of the afternoon suddenly eased dramatically. Raúl, trudging to keep up, cursed fluently in Spanish as the going became much rougher.

Samantha sat wearily before Ross, accepting the support of his chest against her back only because she was too exhausted to do anything else. Her eyes, bloodshot from lack of sleep and the awful glare of the sun, were never still.

Escape. The need for it ate at her, twisting her stomach into a sickening knot. But as they traveled farther into the interior, it looked less and less likely.

The lonely howl of the wind whispered through the mountains; the only sounds of humanity were the creaking of the saddle and Raúl's angry mutterings.

The rest stops were few now and offered little chance for escape. Her captors watched her like a hawk. Ross's eyes were sardonic, amused, alert, as he patiently waited for her to make a move. But it was Raúl with his oily smile and hot gleaming eyes, who made her skin crawl. She shivered and wrapped her arms about herself as twilight slowly, persistently approached, but the coldness that licked at her came from within. Apprehension threatened to choke her. What did these men intend to do with her?

Ross felt her shiver and steeled himself to ignore it. She was tough, he told himself in irritation. Any woman who could survive what she had today without falling to pieces wouldn't bat an eye at finding herself alone with two men in the mountains after dark. She couldn't break now; he wouldn't let her.

The mare, suddenly scenting home, increased her pace and made her way unerringly through the now thick brush that protected the smugglers' hideout at the top of the ridge. Ross heaved a sigh of relief as the house came into sight. Just as soon as the opportunity presented itself, he'd find a way for Red to escape. Then she'd be on her own, and he could finally forget about her and concentrate on his job.

The mare trotted into an overgrown clearing that had once been the yard of someone's home, and Samantha brightened at the first sign of civilization she had seen all day. A house, outbuildings, a barn. Maybe someone here could help her.

But a second look sent her hopes crashing to the ground. She stiffened as Ross brought the horse to a stop in front of a ramshackle building that looked as if it were standing thanks only to the grace of God. The gray, warped wooden siding hadn't seen a coat of paint in the past twenty years, the tin roof was rusty and the porch defied gravity to lean at a precarious angle. In spite of that, a handful of men lounged on the rotten steps and porch, their worn, hopeless faces brightening at the sight of Raúl and Ross. Wets waiting to cross. Samantha blinked back the hot sting of tears. There would be no help coming from them.

"Home, sweet home," Ross said wryly as he swung down from the saddle and turned to help her dismount. At the sight of her contemptuous glance, he grinned and placed his hands more firmly around her waist. "Come on, Red, don't look at me like that. I'll think you don't like the accommodations."

"How perceptive of you," she said dryly, desperately trying to ignore the way her heart jumped in her breast at his touch. It was fear, she told herself as she jerked out of his hold once her feet hit the rocky ground. She was at his mercy, and they both knew it. But she'd be damned if she'd tremble at his touch! "If I have to associate with a pack of rats, I prefer the four-legged kind."

His gray eyes danced. "Oh, they're here, too. So you should have no cause for complaint." He grabbed the reins of the mare and turned to Raúl. "While I'm bedding down the mare, you can show our visitor where the kitchen is. She might as well make herself useful and cook us something to eat."

"No!" Panic streaked through Samantha at the thought of going anywhere with Raúl. He had been watching her all day, his dark eyes secretive, lecherous, stripping her naked countless times, the slight smile that pulled at his mouth always cruel. Her stomach turned. He was just waiting to get her alone; she could see it in his eyes. "I'm not your slave. If you're hungry, you can do your own cooking."

"That wasn't a request, *señorita*," Raúl retorted silkily, the glint in his black eyes dangerous as he stepped toward her. "It was an order."

Samantha's blood ran cold; her throat suddenly felt as dry as the desert wind. Silently he dared her to defy him, and she knew she was going to accept that dare. She had no other choice. She glared at Ross, unaware of the way her eyes appealed to him for help. "What are you going to do if I refuse? Beat me?"

"Don't tempt me, Red," he warned her softly. Damn it, why did she have to pick now to make a stand! She was afraid of Raúl—any woman in her right mind *would* be afraid of the smuggler—but he wasn't going to leave her alone with him that long. If she would just trust him... Ross swore softly. Hell, after what she'd been through, why should she? he thought in disgust.

"Let me put it this way," he replied quietly, dangerously. "You know we're not going to kill you without orders from *El Chiso*. But we can make life so uncomfortable for you you'll wish you were dead. Now are you going to do as you're told or not?"

Samantha lifted her chin at the threat, impotent fury turning her eyes to hard, brilliant sapphires and the taste of defeat bitter on her tongue. Hurt twisted her heart, surprising her. Idiot! she cried silently, stiffening. Had she actually expected him to understand? To protect her from Raúl? He was his partner, for God's sake! And in spite of the fact that he had seemed to watch over her while they were in the desert, he was a hard man, little better than his sleezy friend. She'd be a fool to forget that.

She was on her own, at their mercy. It was a damnable position, but if she wanted to get out of here alive, her only choice was to antagonize her captors as little as possible. She'd wait for them to relax their guard and for L.J. to make his way back to the station. Mac would send someone to help her. He had to.

In spite of the questionable safety of the porch, she made her way up the steps before turning to confront her two captors, her back ramrod straight. "You win this round. I'll cook your stupid food. But I hope you choke on it!"

Ross grinned and started for the barn. "I thought you'd see things my way, Red."

Raúl's soft chuckle infuriated her, but Samantha didn't even bother to look at him. Their day would come, and then she would be the one laughing, she promised herself as she jerked open the screen door and stepped inside.

The impetuosity of her anger carried her halfway across the room before she stopped short, alarm bells suddenly clanging in her head as booted footsteps followed her. The sun had dipped behind the mountains, shrouding the house in a concealing cloak of darkness. Impatiently Samantha willed her eyes to adjust to the dim light as icy fingers of fear seemed to walk down her spine. The house was quiet, too quiet. And she was alone in it with Raúl.

She swallowed nervously, tensing for the attack she knew was sure to come. The men on the porch were within easy calling distance, but she wouldn't even waste her breath appealing to them for help. They were waiting to cross the river; they wouldn't risk losing that opportunity for her.

Raúl's hot breath suddenly caressed her nape, startling a frightened gasp out of her. She whirled like a cornered animal and backed away, her blue eyes wide and wary in the darkness, her heart pounding frantically in her breast. Her chances of besting him were slim to none, but she couldn't let him touch her. Not without a fight.

The strike of a match was loud in the frightening silence. Raúl bent to light a kerosene lamp that sat in the center of a scarred table, his smile distorted and wicked in the flickering flame as his eyes snared hers. *"Mi casa es su casa,"* he purred huskily.

My house is your house. Samantha snorted in contempt and shriveled him with a glance. "Your generosity is overwhelming. Especially since I'm here under protest."

"Don't be difficult, *señorita*. Why make it hard on yourself?" His hot eyes swept over her suggestively before slowly returning to her face. "You're a very passionate woman. If you weren't so busy fighting us, you might enjoy yourself."

Revulsion rose like bile in her throat. "Don't flatter yourself," she said flatly.

His teeth flashed in a smooth, slick smile that never reached his eyes. "With a little effort, perhaps I can change your mind."

Fear slithered over her, and it took every ounce of control she possessed not to back away from him in terror. This was a man who thrived on a woman's fears and weaknesses, who wouldn't hesitate to exploit them for his own amusement. At the first sign of panic, he'd be on her like a starving man on a candy bar. Frantically she searched for an escape.

The main room of the house served as both kitchen and living room, and even by the weak light of the lamp, she could see that the furnishings were poor. A battered sofa was pushed up against one wall, its once-red upholstery hardly recognizable beneath years of dirt and countless stains. The table and a motley collection of wooden chairs sat in the middle of the room, and against another wall stood a huge black cast-iron wood cook stove. The windows were bare of curtains, the floors rugless. Near the stove was a built-in counter with a sink and old-fashioned hand pump for water.

No electricity. No gas. And no means of escape other than the front door.

Distract him, her mind hissed. Buy yourself some time. It was her only hope.

Her gaze riveted on the old stove. It was a hundred years old if it was a day, and as foreign to her as a microwave would be to the pioneers. She felt Raúl's eyes on her and turned her attention back to him. "I can't cook on that," she said unequivocally. "I don't even know how to light it."

His smile was slow, menacing. "Ah, but you will, *señorita*. Come, I'll show you." And before she could object, he grabbed her arm and pulled her closer to the stove. "It's really quite easy. All you have to do is build a fire in the firebox and you're ready to cook."

Samantha's gaze fell to his fingers, then to his nails that were jagged and unkept, encrusted with dirt. Her stomach turned. Just the thought of them touching her was enough to make her break out in a cold sweat. She jerked away with the pretext of getting wood from the woodbox that sat next to the stove. "I'm sure I can figure it out," she told him as she reached for some kindling. "Just tell me what you want cooked. You don't have to watch me."

"But I like watching you," he countered smoothly, his eyes devouring her. "Here, let me help you." But instead of reaching for the wood, his fingers closed around her waist.

She gasped, furious with herself for being so careless. Raúl Sandoval was not the type of man a woman turned her back on. With a muttered curse she whirled to face him. And caught him squarely in the gut with a sharp piece of pine.

The sound of ripping cloth was like a scream in the sudden ominous silence.

For one heart-stopping moment she was afraid he would strike her. The light in his dark eyes was fierce, his sardonic smile now a snarl. His fingers tightened ever so slightly at her waist before he pushed her away, his expression harsh. "Light the fire *señorita*." He jabbed at a compartment on the left side of the stove, next to the oven. "Here."

Her heart thundering in her breast, Sam prayed he couldn't hear her knees knocking as she turned to stuff the wood into the stove. She'd have liked to stuff him into the firebox! Where the hell was Ross?

"Now open all the vents." When she looked at him blankly, he motioned to several places on the back and side of the stove. "The fire can't burn without air," he told her contemptuously.

An angry retort trembled on Sam's lips, but she wisely clamped her teeth on it. She wouldn't let him taunt her into doing something stupid. "All right," she said stiffly, "they're open. Now what?"

"Light the fire."

The kindling was dry and quickly went up in flames. She watched in satisfaction as it caught before she slowly, reluctantly, turned to face Raúl. "If you'll show me where the food is kept..."

"In a minute," he rasped, closing the distance between them in two long strides. "You have lit one fire, now you can put out another."

Her breath jammed in her throat. Unwittingly she automatically backed away, but there was no where to go. Raúl stood between her and the door, and behind her was the hot stove. "Stop it!" she snapped, angrily slapping at his arms as they attempted to wrap around her. "Get your hands off of me!"

His dark black eyes glinted fiercely. "So you want to play rough. My pleasure, *señorita*." And with a lightning-swift lunge, he grabbed her braid and jerked her against him. When she screamed, he only laughed insolently and swept one hand down the slight curves of her body, molding her to him while his other hand kept a tight, cruel pressure on her hair. "I don't think you'll fight me now, *señorita*."

"Don't bet on it!" she countered, revolted by the feel of his hot breath on her face and his hands on her body. Damn him! Did he actually think she would just stand there and let him rape her? She brought her booted foot down smartly on his. He grunted in pain, his hold on her hair loosening ever so slightly, and with a final kick to his shin, she was free. She scurried around the table and picked up the first weapon that came to hand. The kerosene lamp.

"You come one step closer, mister, and you really will be hot," she whispered hoarsely.

Raúl hesitated, frustrated anger hardening the lines of his face. "I don't think you have the guts to throw that, *señorita*."

"Take another step and find out," she taunted.

The screen door suddenly squeaked in protest as Ross jerked it open and stepped inside. His alert eyes quickly comprehended the situation, and he made no attempt to hold back a sardonic grin. "Looks like you're losing your touch, Raúl," he drawled as he casually leaned back against the doorjamb and crossed his arms over his chest. "Red seems to have gotten the upper hand here."

A muscle ticked along Raúl's tightly clenched jaw. "Get the lamp, *amigo*, and then we'll see who has the upper hand."

Ross's grin only widened. "Sorry to disappoint you, but you're going to have to save the fun and games for later. Something's wrong with the pump outside and there's no water for the horses. You better go look at it before it's too dark to see.''

A string of Spanish curses turned the air blue. ''You look at it. I have better things to do.''

''I'm sure you do,'' Ross said with a chuckle. ''But that pump is your baby. You know I don't know a damn thing about it.''

Samantha stood stiffly, her fingers tight around the lamp as Raúl's hard eyes raked over her. ''All right,'' he snarled to Ross. ''I'll look at it.'' His gaze swung back to Sam. ''Don't think this is the end of this, *se- ñorita*. You will live to regret threatening me.''

He stormed out without waiting for a response, leaving behind a tense silence. Samantha felt Ross move behind her, and whirled in alarm, the lamp held high. Ross watched her warily, noting the desperation that clouded her eyes, the defiant lift of her rounded chin, the slight shaking of her arms as she held the lamp aloft. She was a gutsy little thing, he thought with a slight smile. And he didn't doubt for a minute that she'd throw the lamp at him if he made one wrong move.

''That must be getting heavy,'' he said quietly as he cautiously made his way to the table and pulled out a chair. ''Why don't you put it down before you drop it and set fire to the house. You won't need it, now that Raúl is outside.''

''You don't expect me to believe that, do you?'' she scoffed. ''You're not any better than he is.''

His grin flashed teasingly. ''Oh, I don't know about that. If I wanted you, a little kerosene lamp wouldn't stop me.'' And before she could begin to guess his intentions, he reached across the table and snatched the lamp out of her hands. He set it on the table and lifted dancing eyes to hers. "See?"

"I'll fight you," she whispered, tears of fear and exhaustion glistening in her eyes as she backed away from him. "I might not have a chance in hell, but I'll fight you."

"Wouldn't you rather use that energy to cook us something to eat? I don't know about you, but I'm starving." At her suspicious look, he chuckled. "For food, Red. Nothing more." He eased into the chair he had pulled out and stretched his long legs under the table, as if he didn't have a care in the world. "What's for supper?"

Samantha eyed him suspiciously, unconvinced. "Do rats eat their own kind?"

His smile was slow, appreciative, softening the hard angles of his face. "Sorry, Red, but we don't keep fresh meat here. No electricity. And rats don't come canned. Looks like you'll have to think of something else." He motioned to a cupboard next to the sink. "Look in there. There's bound to be something interesting."

Could she trust him enough to turn her back on him? Her eyes searched his face for the cunning she had seen in Raúl's, but it wasn't there. He was relaxed, unperturbed by her suspicions, his only interest at the moment food. He had no intention of taking up where Raúl had left off. At least not until he had had something to eat.

Tears of relief threatened, horrifying her. Blindly she turned toward the cupboard, hardly seeing its meager contents as she sought for control. Conflicting emotions flailed her as she dragged in a shuddering breath. Resentment, anger, gratitude. Damn it, what was wrong with her? She should hate and despise Ross, not feel grateful, for God's sake! He was the one who had captured her, knocked her out, convinced the others to take her and L.J. prisoner. He didn't care about her. He just hadn't wanted to incur *El Chiso*'s wrath. After supper, he'd probably turn her back over to Raúl without batting an eye.

Resentment flared. She grabbed several cans, only to stop just short of banging them down on the counter. Her eyes narrowed thoughtfully as she weighed them in her hands.

"Don't even think it," Ross growled. "Even if you did get past me—which you wouldn't—Raúl would be waiting for you outside. And believe me, Red, you don't want to be alone with him again. He doesn't forget a threat."

Samantha set the cans down sharply and turned to glare at him. "My name is Samantha, not Red! And you can save your subtle warnings for someone who'll appreciate them. You'll never let me out of here alive, so I've got nothing to lose by trying to escape."

"Raúl wouldn't be content with just killing you," he replied softly, dangerously.

"I know." But she couldn't think of that. She couldn't afford the luxury of fear. Silently she cursed the shaking of her limbs, and lifted her chin. "How many people am I supposed to be cooking for?"

Ross hesitated, reluctantly letting her change the subject. She was too stubborn for her own good. He only hoped she waited until he was in a position to help her before she made a break for it. "Manuel probably won't make it back tonight, so with the wets outside, there'll be eight of us," he finally answered. "Need some help?"

"No. It doesn't take two to make canned beans."

What she really wanted was for him to go away, but she knew that was impossible. She turned her back on him and searched the cabinets for a pot, constantly aware of his eyes on her. They wandered over her lazily, stroking her in an almost physical caress that left her hot, breathless, aching. The heat that climbed into her cheeks had nothing to do with sunburn.

"Ever cook on a wood stove before?" Ross asked casually, his gaze lingering on the sweet curve of her bottom as she bent down to look in the back of one of the lower cabinets.

"No."

"You haven't lived until you've tasted biscuits baked in a wood stove. You know how to make biscuits from scratch?"

"No."

Laughter tugged at Ross's mouth. "You're a talkative little thing, aren't you?"

Samantha clamped her teeth on a scathing retort and set the pot of beans on one of the stove's six eyes. "I'm not a 'little thing,'" she said tightly. "And you can hardly expect me to be chatty with my kidnappers."

"No, I guess not," he said, unperturbed by her coldness. "If you don't want to talk, we'll have to find something else to pass the time. What would you be doing if you were home tonight? Spending it with your lover?''

"That's none of your business!''

"Oh, I don't know about that," he argued, his gray eyes dancing. "If you're used to having a man in your bed, we wouldn't want you to go without just because you're not home tonight. Why, I'd even volunteer to be of service.''

The teasing, the taunting, was suddenly too much. How much did they expect her to take? she wondered wildly. "You...you son of a bitch!" she cried, snatching up an iron skillet from the counter and turning to confront him. "You lay a hand on me, and you'll live to regret it.''

The chair Ross was sitting on went crashing to the floor as he surged to his feet, and Samantha hardly had time to note the cold fury on his face before she found herself pinned against the wall by his body, his fingers manacling her wrists on either side of her head. "Let's leave my mother out of this," he growled softly.

The quietness of his voice drained the blood out of her cheeks. He had the infinite patience of a hunter waiting to strike, watching his quarry with gray eyes that were as cold as the Arctic. This was a man who wouldn't hesitate to kill if he felt threatened. Slowly, persistently, his fingers tightened around her wrists, until she dropped the skillet with a cry of pain.

Her eyes locked with his. He was close, too close, his unwavering gaze seeming to peer into her very soul. Was that her heart thundering in her breast or his? His face was only a hairbreadth away from hers, his breath a whispered promise against her lips, heating them, seducing them. Suddenly she was achingly aware of every hard male inch of him pressed intimately against her, the taut, unyielding strength of his thigh wedged between her legs, the granite smoothness of his chest crushing her breasts. The pounding of her pulse quickened, echoing a heat that throbbed deep inside her, stunning her. Oh, God, she was practically melting in his arms!

Ross realized he'd made a mistake almost immediately. He never should have touched her. Need curled into his loins, hot, fierce, surprising him with its intensity. He swore softly, fighting for control. What the hell was wrong with him? She was nothing but a redheaded witch with a tongue that could cut to the quick. Yet he wanted her. Sunburned, dirty, her hair a tangled mess, he didn't care. He ached to have her in his bed, her feminine softness sliding under him, over him, surrounding him with the heat and passion lurking in her eyes. He was tempted, damn tempted, to make her admit she wanted the same thing. He shifted his grip from her wrist to her hands, his fingers intertwining with hers, his hungry gaze drawn to the sensuous, inviting curve of her lips. One kiss, he promised himself. A taste.

Trapped, Samantha watched his dark head descend as if she were mesmerized. She felt bombarded by an array of conflicting emotions that left her helpless in his grasp. "No!" she whispered hoarsely, struggling against the desire that pulled at her like an undertow. The acrid scent of scalded beans drifted

SHADOWS IN THE NIGHT

toward her, and she grabbed at the pot like a lifeline. "The beans! They're burning."

Ross stiffened, his nostrils flaring, every muscle in his body tightening in protest. For what seemed like an eternity he stared into her eyes, to see the same desire that ate at him and a fear that left him cold. He swore softly under his breath and released her.

"This is your last warning, Red," he snarled. "Next time you try something stupid I'm going to tie you up."

He strode quickly across the room and threw himself on the couch to glare at her, his angry scowl daring her to say one word in protest.

Pale and shaken, Samantha leaned weakly against the wall and fought a ridiculous urge to cry. Furiously she blinked back the betraying tears and forced herself to move, ignoring the still thunderous pounding of her heart and the man who watched her with icy gray eyes.

She moved like an automaton, using a rag as a potholder as she rescued the beans with an economy of movement, hardly noticing the stove's heat, her eyes blank, concealing. But inside she seethed with an urgency that bordered on panic. She had to get away. Tonight. Before she ended up in Ross de la Garza's bed.

The screen door slammed. Startled, Samantha looked up to find Raúl's narrowed black eyes devouring her. The men who were waiting to cross the river stood at his back. His smile held the promise of revenge. "We're hungry, *señorita*. How much longer are you going to keep us waiting?"

Ross tensed as the other man's eyes insolently ran over Samantha. If Raúl laid so much as a finger on her, he'd knock his head off!

And blow the lid off your cover, a mocking voice in his head reminded him. Don't be a jackass!

With the utmost care, Ross uncurled his clenched fingers and leaned back, his arms outstretched along the back of the couch. "Get the pump fixed?"

"Yeah," the smuggler replied, his eyes still on Samantha. "Tomorrow I'll show you how to fix it, then I can stay and keep the *señorita* company."

Tomorrow, God willing, she would be long gone. With a satisfying thud, she sat the pot of beans on the table and lifted defiant eyes to Raúl. "The food's ready."

"You must go first, *señorita*." He laughed softly, cunningly. "Just to make sure you do not poison us." The men standing behind him, obviously not understanding, made a move toward the table. With an angry growl, Raúl stopped them in their tracks and with a mocking bow motioned Samantha to precede them. *"Señorita?"*

She would have loved to throw his gallantry in his face and damn the consequences, but common sense wisely held her temper in check. She had to eat. If she ever escaped from here, the next meal would be many miles away. Without a word, she retrieved a spoon and tin plate from those she had set out on the counter and served herself a generous portion of beans.

The others soon followed suit, quickly finding places to sit at the table and on the couch before digging into their food. Samantha watched in chagrin as the aliens wolfed down the burned beans as if they hadn't eaten in days. They probably hadn't.

Suddenly sick at heart, she offered the remaining portion of her food to a pathetically thin old man who had come back for seconds and found the pot empty. When he looked at her in surprise, she smiled and pushed it into his hands. "Take it," she told him in Spanish. "I've had enough."

More than enough. Of the food, her surroundings, her captors. How could anyone eat, she wondered, when the tension in the house was thick enough to choke a horse? Raúl was just waiting for his revenge, watching her every move as if she were a helpless mouse he could toy with before he pounced on her like a cat. And Ross just sat there, watching, waiting. But for what?

One by one, the aliens set their empty plates in the sink and went outside, presumably to the barn that was within a stone's throw of the house. The silence fairly screamed at her as she watched them leave. Her eyes darted to the door and escape, before shifting back to Raúl. He set his fork in his empty plate and stared pointedly at her, a half smile mocking her. Helplessly Samantha felt her nerves stretch to the breaking point as fear crawled into her stomach and sickened her. Could she make it to the door before he caught her?

Ross lounged negligently on the couch in pretended unconcern, his gray eyes narrowed and dangerous beneath half-closed lids as he watched the drama unfolding before him. He called himself seven kinds of a fool for caring whether Raúl tried to take Samantha to bed. He had a responsibility to get her out of here alive. Nothing else. He knew that, accepted it. But if anyone was going to take her, it would be him.

Adrenaline surged through him as he watched Raúl come to his feet. As if he hadn't a care in the world, Ross leaned back against the back of the couch, his muscles tensed to spring, his eyes trained unwaveringly on the other man. "You can forget what you're thinking, Raúl," he drawled. "She's mine."

Chapter Four

Hostility suddenly crackled in the air like raw electricity. Though softly spoken, Ross's words landed like a thrown gauntlet at Raúl's booted feet, daring him to accept the challenge, daring him to be so foolish as to take another step toward Samantha. Time ceased to exist as a thick, cold cloud of silence hovered over the room. No one moved.

Samantha's breath lodged somewhere in her throat, relief coursing through her, turning her knees to butter. Ross wasn't going to let Raúl touch her. Did he know that just the thought of Raúl's hands on her was enough to make her gag?

She's mine.

His words were lazy, confident, possessive. He was actually *claiming* her, Samantha realized, suddenly outraged. Who the hell did he think he was? she fumed, glaring at him. This wasn't the Dark Ages! He couldn't just drag her off to his bed like he owned her. Nobody owned her!

Her narrowed gaze spit daggers, impaling his form to the couch. What a fool she was to expect any sort of decency from him. He wasn't saving her from Raúl out of the goodness of his heart. The snake didn't have a heart! He wanted her for himself.

Fury seethed through her, and for one sweet moment she was tempted to wipe that infuriating half smile off his face. But his strength was far superior to hers, and he'd never let her get away with it. "I don't belong to you or any other man," she shot back angrily.

"You don't have any say in the matter. This is between Raúl and me, so keep out of it."

"No say!" she sputtered indignantly. "I've got a hell of a lot to say about this!"

"You must be joking, *amigo*," Raúl interrupted, puzzled amusement sliding across his swarthy face. His lips curled in disdain as his gaze fell on Samantha. "She is not worth fighting for."

Ross lifted a dark brow, his slow smile mocking. "You think so? Then we have nothing to argue about. She's mine."

"You twist my words," Raúl protested silkily, his black eyes cagey. "She is nothing but a *gringa*. There is no reason we can't share."

"I don't share what is mine. Sorry, *amigo*."

The smaller man stiffened at the mimicking retort, and the rancid scent of danger was suddenly strong in the air. A threat of ugliness crept into the room on invisible feet.

Samantha paled and told herself she didn't care if they killed each other. They were nothing but animals, anyway, vultures waiting to pick the bones of their victims. If she could just slip away while they were fighting...

But what if Raúl won? The unwanted thought stopped her before she'd done more than gauge the distance to the door, chilling her to the bone. Raúl would come after her. And when he caught her... A shiver of revulsion ran down her spine. He would make her pay dearly for her defiance.

And if Ross won? Unconsciously her eyes lingered on him, a soft flush flooding her cheeks as heat coiled into her stomach. He was a good six inches taller than Raúl, leaner, stronger. And far more dangerous. With just a touch he could make her body play traitor to her mind. She, who had never drooled over a man in her life, had found herself nearly melting at his feet. Did he have any idea how that terrified her?

Yet he was definitely the lesser of two evils. Somehow she had to stop them from coming to blows.

"I wish you two could see yourselves," she said scathingly, stepping between them. "You look ridiculous! I wouldn't have either one of you on a silver platter, so if you're doing this to impress me, you can stop right now."

"Shut up, Samantha," Ross growled harshly, his gaze trained on Raúl. "Get over by the stove and stay out of this."

He called her "Samantha," she thought inanely, ridiculously pleased at the sound of her name on his lips. For once he wasn't mocking her. Maybe she could make him see reason. "Ross, this isn't necessary—"

"Move, damn it!"

She jumped at his angry roar, her mouth dry, her eyes wide and startled as she slowly, carefully, backed up. From the corner of his eye, Ross watched her retreat until the countertop dug into the small of her back. Only then did he allow himself to release the breath he had been holding. One of these days, he promised himself, he was going to teach her to obey an order without arguing!

The flame of the lamp flickered, teased by a draft. From beneath craggy brows, Ross watched Raúl as if he were a rattler threatening to strike. I'm in a hell of a mess now, he thought cynically, and all because of a woman. He cursed softly. Damn her and his suddenly active conscience! If he didn't play this very carefully, his cover was going to be shot to hell.

He came to his feet with the lazy grace of a stretching mountain lion, the smile that hovered around his mouth at odds with the alert bite of his eyes as they snared his opponent's. "She's mine, Raúl. After what she put me through today, don't you think I'm entitled? The little wildcat tried to drown me in the river! This is my chance to pay her back."

"She threatened me, *amigo*." His black eyes were cold, bottomless, as they turned on Samantha. "I, too, want revenge."

"Then you can kill her when the orders come from *El Chiso*," Ross replied flatly. "Until then, she's mine."

"And if I disagree?"

"Then you'll have to take her from me. If you think you're big enough."

Raúl stiffened at the softly issued challenge. He was tempted—Ross could see it in his eyes. The smuggler was small—nearly thirty pounds lighter—and quick. And he wouldn't hesitate to fight dirty...a kick to the groin or a switchblade pulled out of a boot could quickly even up the odds. Ross had come up against his kind countless times in the past eighteen years—small, cocky men who lived in the shadows and played by their own rules. They very seldom had the guts to confront an adversary openly. And they never forgot a slight, regardless of how small or insignificant it was.

Raúl hesitated, then suddenly relaxed, a furtive gleam glistening in his black eyes as he flashed Ross a reproachful grin. "So serious, *amigo*! You want the woman? She is yours. Enjoy!"

"I thought you'd see things my way," Ross said lightly, the tough, grim lines around his mouth stretching into an easy smile that held no trace of the tenseness that still gripped him. Raúl didn't fool him for a moment. He was conceding only until the odds were more in his favor, and they both knew it. Ross turned to Samantha, his pale eyes once again mocking. "Into the bedroom, Red," he ordered, motioning to a closed door to his left. "It's beddy-bye time."

The blood drained from Samantha's face. "No!"

"Oh, yes," he rasped. "I've waited all day for this. Are you going to go peacefully, or do I have to carry you?"

A broken sob choked her as her eyes darted between the two men and the only door that led to escape. Too late! her heart cried. She had waited too long. Dear God, what now?

Don't panic. Hysterical laughter welled in her at the thought. Don't panic? How could she not? She was terrified!

Her nails bit into her palms. The small, stinging pain gradually penetrated the fear that fogged her mind, and a calming breath tore through her. Slowly, deliberately, she unclenched her fingers. She had to keep her wits about her. It was her only hope.

She lifted her chin and started for the bedroom without saying another word, the burning anger of her eyes the only show of emotion on her cold face. Ross stopped her before she could take more than a few steps. "Here," he said, tossing her the book of matches he'd dredged out of his shirt pocket. "Light the candle on the dresser. I like to see what I'm getting."

If she'd had a gun then, she could have shot him without a twinge of remorse. She had to be content, instead, with just catching the matches and not even deigning to answer him. In comparison, they offered little satisfaction.

Ross watched the bedroom door shut behind her stiff figure and knew a momentary twinge of regret. He'd never treated a woman so shabbily in his life! But what could he do but play the part Raúl expected of him? The least sign of softness or concern for her welfare would raise suspicions he'd have a hard time explaining. Cursing under his breath, he turned to playfully slap the smuggler on the back. "Come on, Raúl, let's have a drink. I've got a feeling I'm going to need it before this night is over."

Raúl's laugh was low, lecherous. "The *señorita* is a fighter. If you need any help, just call."

Samantha shut the door sharply and leaned against it as their every word easily carried to her through the paper-thin bedroom wall. A shiver crawled over her icy skin; the fear she had tried to hold at bay for hours fed on the darkness that enveloped her. Terror suddenly engulfed her. It undermined her defenses until it gagged her. How long before he joined her? she wondered wildly. How long before he raped her?

Her blood congealed at the thought. No! Denial screamed through her. She couldn't, wouldn't, let him do this to her. She had to get away!

With trembling fingers, she pulled a match from the matchbook and struck it, her eyes quickly scanning the room in the few seconds she had before it went out.

The room was small—ten by ten, at the most—with one window and bare but for the necessities. A rickety oak dresser sat against one wall, its mirror splotched and cracked, the candle Ross had spoken of stuck on a small saucer that sat on one corner of the dresser top. Against the opposite wall stood an iron bed. Samantha cringed at the sight of it. It was unmade, the rumpled sheets yellowed and dirty, clinging to a tired-looking mattress that sagged in the middle. An army blanket dragged the dusty wood floor.

She struck another match, her hand cupping the flame protectively as she made her way to the dresser and lit the candle. She winced at the sight of the woman who stared back at her from the mirror. Her eyes were dark pools of desperation in a face that was colorless but for the bright spots of sunburn on her cheeks. She looked haggard, drawn, overwrought.

A cold wind whistled around the windowsill. She froze, her eyes drawn to the eerie sound. The blackness of the night stared back at her through the uncurtained window.

Her heart thundered against her ribs like a jackhammer. The window! Had they forgotten about it? She rushed over and jerked at the sash, but it refused to budge. A sob rose in her throat. No! she cried silently, desperation giving her added strength as she pushed at the wooden frame. It had to open!

"You're wasting your time, Red. It's nailed shut."

Her face went ashen at the sound of the familiar lazy drawl. Her eyes dropped to the bottom of the window frame, where two rusty nail heads were firmly embedded. An anger unlike any she had ever known surged through her, and with an outraged cry she turned to face him, her eyes blazing. "You touch me," she vowed in a voice that dripped icicles, "and so help me God, I'll make you regret it!"

"I don't think so," Ross retorted with a wicked grin, his arms crossed over his chest as he leaned against the door. The weak light thrown off by the candle barely reached him, casting his bearded face in shadows.

From beneath craggy brows, his pale gray eyes roamed over her at will and missed little. "Ah, Red, I don't think I could ever regret touching you."

Samantha shrank against the wall. "Are you so desperate for a woman that you have to force yourself on me?"

His dark brows lowered in a fierce frown. "Do you think I'd be here if I could stay away?" he growled. Damn it, he didn't have any choice in the matter! He had to do what was expected of him.

Oh, come off it, man, a cynical voice in his head jeered. You've been dreaming of getting her in your bed ever since you met her.

It was true, he silently admitted, frustration clenching his jaw. But not like this. After tonight she'd hate his guts. If she didn't already. He swore softly and pushed himself away from the door. This would be a hell of a lot easier if she weren't so easy to touch.

Samantha stiffened as he moved toward her on silent feet, stalking her. Her heart skidded to her knees before shooting back up to her chest. "I'll fight you," she whispered hoarsely. "And if I can, I'll hurt you."

"I'm shaking in my shoes," he taunted, his teeth flashing in amusement. He took the final step that brought him directly in front of her, his blue eyes intense, hard, as they snared hers. "Scream," he said softly.

She gasped as if he'd struck her, her freckles standing out in bold relief against her bloodless cheeks. Oh, God, what kind of pervert was he? She cringed, though he made no move to touch her. "No," she croaked.

"Don't make me force you," he rasped. "You'll regret it. Now scream, damn you!"

"Why? Does fear turn you on?"

His eyes narrowed to mere slits. "And if it does?"

"I wouldn't scream if my life depended on it."

"It just might," Ross muttered angrily, and reached for her.

She was so small, he thought in surprise as his fingers closed around her upper arms. She was always so tough, that until he touched her he tended to forget just how fragile she was. And then his hands seemed to swallow her, his fingers easily encircling her wrist, her waist. She was soft, like satin; he could feel the softness of her even through her dusty green uniform. And beneath her delicate exterior was a brittle tension that was on the edge of breaking.

Ross watched her bite her lower lip as she stubbornly refused any kind of protest that might give him satisfaction. Her blue eyes were nearly violet with fear, and he muttered a bitter curse. He wanted to hold her, to kiss her, to take that look from her eyes. But he couldn't. Not yet.

A muscle ticked in his jaw as he deliberately ran his hands up her arms to her shoulders. With painstaking slowness his fingers traced her collarbone through the material of her shirt. His misty gray eyes trapped hers, taunting her when he reached for the first button on her blouse. He toyed with it, hating himself when she whimpered in terror, despising himself when she flinched as he released the button from its buttonhole and moved on to the next.

She was frozen with fear, her skin like ice under his fingers. Don't look at me like that! he wanted to cry. Instead he gripped the front of her shirt with both hands and sent the rest of the buttons flying with a savage pull.

Dazed, Samantha stared at his hands as they held her blouse open. In growing horror, she watched his fingers move to the front clasp of her bra, releasing it, moving the lacy cups aside, exposing her to his burning gaze.

He touched her, his rough, callused fingers closing around her, and suddenly it was too much. All the atrocities she had suffered that day closed around her like quicksand, pulling her down into a dark, bottomless nightmare that threatened her very soul. She screamed, a bloodcurdling cry of horror that welled up from the depths of her being.

From the other room, soft, sinister laughter mixed with her screams. *"Muy bien, amigo,"* Raúl called out. "Go for it!"

Regret sickened Ross, and at that moment, if he could have put his fingers around Raúl's throat, he would have shown him no mercy. With a muttered curse, he dragged Samantha into his arms, stopping her painful cries with his mouth.

She fought him with every ounce of her rapidly dwindling strength. Her balled fists plowed into him, striking out at the nightmare that held her in its grip, pummeling the man who had teased and taunted her all day until she just couldn't take any more. Her breath ripped through her lungs, tearing her apart. Her arms were heavy with fatigue, and still she lashed out at him, her sobs muffled against his mouth.

Ross grunted in pain as her blows landed about his face and chest, never lifting a hand to stop her, never lifting his mouth from hers. After what she'd been through today, he wouldn't blame her if she wanted to beat the hell out of him. All he wanted to do was hold her. And make love to her. He groaned deep in his throat, unable to close his mind to the feel of her breasts in his hands, unable to stop himself from pulling her closer, trapping her flailing arms between their bodies.

Samantha moaned in frustration, her arms leaden, immobile. Useless tears rolled down her cheeks. Damn him! Why didn't he get it over with and be done with it?

Her anger rolled over him like a red-hot wave of fury, battering against the invincible wall of his strength, never touching him. But he winced at the taste of her tears on his lips. Tenderness assaulted him, surprising him. Without even realizing it, he soothed her with hands that were suddenly gentle, moving over her with slow deliberation, chasing away her fears, delighting in the feel of her. Even when she struggled against him, blind to his need for her, she made him ache.

His scent surrounded her, a dusty, masculine scent that pierced the panic that shrouded her and slowly, insidiously, attacked her senses. Samantha stiffened, suddenly vulnerable, exposed to a heat that left her weak, an awareness that left her spent, trembling, in his arms. The scratch of his beard was a rough, sensuous caress against her sunburned face, the gentle persuasion of hands that slipped under the remains of her shirt to travel over her naked back no longer threatening, sliding to her waist and back up her spine, warming her, seducing her.

Don't let him do this to you, a voice in her head cried out in outrage. Fight him.

But the sweet, tempting taste of his mouth on hers scattered her thoughts like tumbleweeds before the wind, and the need for escape withered and died without regret. He nibbled at the corners of her mouth, the full, sensual lower lip, teasing her, wooing her, promising untold delights. Her pulse quickened, stealing her breath. At the flick of his tongue, heat streaked through her like summer lightning, racing to her fingertips, dragging pleasure in its wake. Her body throbbed for his touch, his taste.

Passion, thick and heavy, curled into Ross's loins. The feel of her bare breasts pressed against his chest staggered him. He lifted his head suddenly to stare down at her, a ragged breath filling his lungs, his gray eyes turbulent with desire. She was hot, hungry, a woman of fire who moved against him with subtle grace, scorching the very air between them, calling to the need that raged in his blood like a forest fire out of control. His fingers dove into the silky strands of her hair, luxuriating in the feel of them curling around him, capturing him even as he captured her mouth again with his, kissing her deeply, hungrily, exploring her dark, sweet secrets as if he were starving for the taste of her.

But it wasn't enough. She made him ache. Dear God, how she made him ache! He had to have her, all of her, and she was more than willing. With a muffled groan, he tore his lips from hers and swept her up into his arms, crossing to the bed in two long strides.

It was a small bed, hardly big enough to accommodate his long frame, with a lumpy mattress that should have been burned years ago. But as he came down beside her, reaching for her with fingers that surprised him with their shakiness, it felt like heaven.

Outside the bedroom door, booted feet moved quietly, stealthily. In the small bedroom's hushed silence, the sound was like a rifle shot.

Ross froze. Instantly alert, his narrowed eyes trained on the closed door. Raúl, he thought in disgust. How could he have forgotten him? How could he have let Red make him forget the other man's presence? Self-disgust welled in him. He couldn't afford to lose himself in the feel of her, the sweetness of her response. If he was stupid enough to let her get under his skin, he'd lose his objectivity where she was concerned. And that could be dangerous.

His jaw clenched on a string of bitter words, and with his body screaming in protest, he released the woman in his arms as if she'd suddenly developed the plague.

Samantha lifted heavy lids, her blue eyes wide, unguarded, clouded with passion. At his cold, contemptuous stare, horror washed over her. Dear God, what had she done? This man represented everything in the world she abhorred, and she had lost herself in his kiss. No, she had all but given herself to him.

And he despised her for it.

Suddenly cold, exposed, humiliated, she dragged her blouse over her nakedness with trembling fingers and vainly fought the hot sting of tears that gathered in her eyes. The glistening drops welled and spilled over her lashes to slide silently down her reddened cheeks. With a sob, she turned away from him and faced the wall, hugging herself as the trickle of tears turned into an ocean, washing over her in wave after wave of pain.

Remorse hit Ross in the stomach. Bewildered, he reached for her, only to stop just short of touching her. He cursed softly, his frown fierce as he glared at the back of her head. "What the devil's wrong with you? I'm not going to rape you, for God's sake!"

She only cried harder. It wouldn't have been rape and they both knew it.

Her muffled sobs shook her slender frame, stabbing Ross in the heart, and though he cursed himself a thousand times for his weakness, he turned on his side and gathered her to his chest. She didn't fight him; she just lay there in his arms, sobbing her heart out.

Helpless, Ross pulled her closer and murmured reassurances into the wild wonder of her hair, his body fitting around hers spoon fashion, his fingers stroking her, consoling her. Unfamiliar emotions swamped him, stunning him. It had been a long time since a woman's tears had touched him, and that woman had been his mother. He'd never held a woman while she cried, never felt the need to offer comfort. But this woman caught him unaware. He'd expected her to fight, to scratch his eyes out if she could, and she hadn't disappointed him. But it was the softness underneath all her toughness that made him ache. He couldn't take advantage of her, not now when she was so vulnerable. She deserved more than a quick, hot tumble and vulgar, listening ears in the other room.

But how would he find the strength to let her go?

His heat scorched the backs of her legs, the curve of her hips, her back, drying up her tears. Samantha dragged in a shuddering breath and ordered herself to move, to get out of his arms before it was too late. But confusion tied her to the bed as surely as if he had bound and gagged her.

Who was this man who tried to rip her clothes from her one minute and then the next held her with such gentleness while she cried? Tenderness was the last thing she expected from him; he disarmed her with it and she was powerless to stop him. He was a criminal, but the feel of him behind her, surrounding her, protecting her, felt so right.

Had he bewitched her? she wondered drowsily. When he was this close she didn't want to think, didn't want to do anything but cuddle up against him and enjoy his heat. She could never before remember wanting to cuddle with anyone, not even Michael, her ex-fiancé. Least of all Michael, she silently corrected herself. Her independence had proved to be a sore spot with Michael, and he'd spent the duration of their short engagement trying to show her how much stronger he was than she. He would have taken cuddling as a sure sign of weakness.

But with Ross it was somehow right. Instinctively she knew her independence didn't bother him in the least. And in spite of what he was, who he was, her body recognized and welcomed his touch. Somehow she would have to come to terms with that. But not now. She was too tired. Sighing, she settled against the hard, reassuring breadth of his chest.

Ross felt her subtle movements all the way to his knees. He groaned at the exquisite torture, his body hot and hard with need, his control nonexistent. He ground his teeth on a muttered oath, fighting the fire that burned him from the inside out, but when she moved again, her hip unconsciously nudging him, he jumped out of the bed as if he'd been shot from a cannon. Damn her! She'd been horrified by her response to him—he'd seen it in her eyes. Yet she didn't hesitate to lie in his arms once he'd assured her he had no intention of raping her.

Did she think he was made of steel? Didn't she know what she was doing to him when she moved against him? He had to get out of here, before the ache she'd stirred got the better of his good intentions.

Startled, Samantha rolled to her back and watched him head for the door. She frowned. "Why?" she asked softly, not even realizing she'd spoken the word aloud until he stopped in his track and turned back to glare at her. "Why didn't you rape me?" It was what she'd expected, what she'd feared, what he'd led Raúl to believe. Yet he was walking out without hardly touching her.

Ross's face was set, grim, his cool gray eyes emotionless as they pinned her to the bed. "I may be many things," he said softly, "but I'm not a rapist. *When* I make love to you, I'm going to make sure I've got all night to do it and there isn't someone in the next room listening for every sound." He reached for the door handle. "Get some sleep," he ordered huskily, and walked out.

Chapter Five

Stunned, Samantha watched him shut the bedroom door with a sharp click. She didn't know whether to laugh or cry. He wanted her to get some sleep? Surely he was joking? How could she even consider sleep when her body still smoldered from his touch?

She closed her eyes against the needs that hammered at her. She was out of her mind, she decided, as the hysterical laughter that bubbled up in her became dangerously close to a sob. How else could she account for the fact that she lost touch with reality when she was in his arms? He made her forget what he was and who she was. He could make her feel things in a way she'd never known existed. It was wonderful.

Until he stopped touching her. Then unfamiliar doubts assailed her, and she hated them. She'd always known her own mind, seldom had reason to question her judgment. She saw things in black or white. There were no in-betweens. Just as there was no question of what Ross de la Garza was—he was a criminal of the lowest kind.

No! her heart cried. She couldn't accept that. Her *heart* couldn't accept that.

Suddenly restless, she jumped up from the bed and straightened her clothes, her fingers trembling when they came to her buttonless blouse. She shivered, chilled by a cold that seemed to seep into her very soul.

Who was she trying to kid? chided a tiny voice in her head. He was a criminal. A smuggler. And, not inconceivably, a murderer. The angular line of her jaw stiffened as she forced herself to consider the possibilities. He was hard, cynical, ruthless, a rebel who obeyed no man's laws but his own.

She could have despised Ross if that had been all there was to him. But underneath the hard-bitten exterior, the mockery, was a softness, a gentleness, a sense of laughter, that was as unexpected and arresting as a rainbow against a stormy sky. And she'd always had a weakness for the unexpected. She'd have given anything to deny her attraction, but couldn't. How could she pretend it wasn't there, when she'd practically melted at his touch?

Heat climbed into her cheeks. No, she silently amended, she hadn't just melted. She'd dissolved like hot honey and flowed all over him. When was the last time that had happened to her?

Never.

How could she have lived twenty-eight years and never felt that? she wondered wildly.

Oh, she'd tasted passion before. The summer she'd turned eighteen, she'd thought herself madly in love with the mechanic who worked on her mother's car. John. She smiled in wry remembrance. She'd been young and rebellious, and the fact that her brothers had heartily disapproved of John had made him seem all the more attractive. But then she'd gone away to college, and the romance ended as quickly as it had begun.

She'd never been the type of woman who felt incomplete without a man. School, and then her career, had assumed first priority in her life, and she'd never felt the need for anything else. She'd been perfectly content with friends instead of lovers.

Then Michael came into her life. Michael, with his dry wit and brilliant mind, had fascinated her. He'd been only too willing to show her what she'd been missing, but he hadn't wanted a border patrol agent for a wife—or a lover, for that matter. No, she was too wild for him, too adventuresome, and it hadn't taken her long to realize he was right. She couldn't be a docile, contented homebody if her life depended on it. Any man who expected that of her would soon bore her to tears.

Even the passion Michael had stirred in her was tepid compared to what Ross made her feel. He took her out of herself with just a touch, exerting a control over her body she had no choice but to fight. Instinctively she knew that if she gave in, even for an instant, she might never be able to walk away.

And she had to walk away.

Had she misjudged him? Her heart refused to let go of that niggling hope. She wanted to believe, *needed* to believe, she had. That was what scared her. She was on the verge of making what could be the biggest mistake of her life, and there didn't seem to be anything she could do about it. The man who lived behind the hard, unfeeling shell that Ross de la Garza presented to the world would be so easy to love.

She hugged herself against the cold and her own uncertainties, her blue eyes bleak as she took in the starkness of her surroundings. Send help soon, Mac, she silently prayed. Before it's too late.

Her eyes fell on the rumpled bed. Lord, she was tired. How long had it been since she'd slept? Thirty-six hours? Forty? It seemed like forever. If she could just lay down for a while and close her eyes...she grimaced at the yellowed sheets.

Not exactly first-class accommodations, she thought grimly. But at least she didn't have to worry about sharing the bed. For whatever his reasons, Ross seemed content with just misleading Raúl. She didn't think he'd be back tonight, and that was fine with her.

Liar, a voice in her head mocked, but she ignored it. After tugging off her boots, she shrugged out of her slacks and buttonless shirt, dropping them to the dusty floor. An icy wind raced down her naked back, and for a fleeting moment she considered sleeping in her clothes. But they were so full of dirt she'd be miserable. Shivering, she blew out the candle and jumped into bed. The blanket would be enough once she warmed up the sheets, she told herself firmly, and tried to believe it. With a sigh, she dragged the scratchy cover up to her chin and let exhaustion pull her toward sleep.

Suddenly, without warning, the bedroom door banged open. Samantha's eyes flew open; her heart jerked in alarm. Ross stood in the doorway, the light from the kerosene lamp he held carving his bearded face in an expression of wickedness. At the sight of the determined set of his jaw, she paled and scrambled to sit up.

Ross stopped short. She was still awake. He cursed softly and continued into the room, shutting the door behind him with a snap, ignoring her as he set the lamp on the dresser. He didn't have to look at her to know that she clutched the blanket like a shield, all but waiting for him to pounce. A muscle along his jaw ticked ominously. Why the hell couldn't she have been asleep? Maybe then he could have crawled into the bed and turned his back on her. Now it was going to be difficult.

He almost laughed aloud. Difficult? It was going to be impossible. And he had nobody to blame but himself. The minute he'd claimed her as his own, there'd never been any question of where he'd spend the night. Like it or not, they were sharing that bed. He could forget about sleeping, though. Just keeping his hands off her was going to take all his concentration.

His teeth clenched in frustration, he reached for the zipper of his jeans.

The scrape of the metal tab was like a scream in the silent room. Samantha gasped, horrified, and bolted off the bed. Her eyes widened in disbelief. "What do you think you're doing?" she asked, shocked.

Ross's answer was lost at the sight of her. He tried to remember that he was not as bad as the animals he'd been living with for the past two months, but he couldn't think of anything but having her. She was lovely. Clothed only in outrage and her underwear, her hair like fire around her naked shoulders, she was a temptress, a vixen, sweet and wild. He couldn't stop his eyes from roaming over her hungrily. At that moment he wanted nothing more than to pull the bra and panties off her and drag her into his arms, the rest of the world be damned.

She was his. It was only a matter of time before he proved it to her.

The hot, lingering touch of his eyes heated her blood, her breasts, her hips. Suddenly realizing that she was all but naked before him, she blushed and snatched up the army blanket, her blue eyes icy as she glared at him defiantly. Her knees trembled traitorously. "Get out of here!"

Ross grinned mockingly. "No way, lady. I'm going to bed."

"Not with me you're not," she snapped, ignoring the grating roughness of the blanket as she pulled it more closely around her.

"Oh, but I am."

His confidence infuriated her. "I should have known you were too good to be true," she said bitterly. "You don't have the decency God gave a snake."

Damn her and her sharp tongue! Is this the thanks he got for saving her from Raúl? "What did you expect from a *coyote*, Red?'' he taunted. ''Manners? Sorry, but I left mine at the border. Now come on, get into bed like a good girl.''

''If I do, you're sleeping on the floor.''

Ross couldn't help but laugh. She was serious! Devilment winked in his eyes. It was time she realized she was the captive and took orders from him! ''After the day I've had,'' he drawled, ''I have no intention of sleeping on the floor.''

Without batting an eye, he calmly stepped out of his pants.

If only she'd had the sophistication to look him over with a cool, superior smile! Samantha fumed, frustrated. But she didn't. He was a magnificent specimen of a man. Lean, without an ounce of fat to mar his firm body, and with power in the subtle play of his muscles, strength in his long limbs. Unable to stop herself, her eyes moved over the broad expanse of his chest, following the line of dark hair that arrowed down to the white jockey shorts hugging his slim hips. Her heart dropped to her knees.

''Like what you see?'' Ross asked with a chuckle.

Startled, her eyes flew to his, her cheeks hot. Oh, she'd like to stuff that grin down his throat! Did he have to notice *everything*? She whirled, her back as straight and unbending as a steel rod. ''I'll take the floor,'' she said tightly. ''It couldn't be any dirtier than the bed.''

But she'd hardly taken a step away from him, when steellike fingers grabbed her. She cried out, startled, her breath leaving her lungs in a rush as she found herself tossed upon the bed. Ross stood over her, his hands planted firmly at his hips, the glint in his gray eyes daring her to make a move.

"Like it or not, Red, you're sleeping with me," he told her fiercely. "I'm not giving you a chance to escape during the night."

He saw the fear that flickered in her eyes and clenched his teeth in frustration. Didn't she know he'd like nothing better than for her to sleep on the floor? Maybe then he'd get some rest. But he couldn't take the chance. If Raúl walked in and found her there, neither one of them would ever see the good old U.S.A. again.

"How could I escape?" she asked in a voice that was anything but steady. "I can't get out the window, and Raúl's in the next room."

"Knowing you, you'd find a way." He tossed her the blanket that had fallen off the bed, then turned to extinguish the lamp. He pulled off his boots and they hit the floor with a loud thump. "Damn, it's cold in here," he growled in the sudden blackness that enveloped them. "Move over."

The order slid over her like a caress. Samantha felt her heart knock against her ribs, and could do nothing to stop it. Slowly, reluctantly, she moved, making room for him beside her.

The mattress sagged, catching her off guard. With a soft gasp she suddenly rolled against him. His naked flesh seared hers from her breasts to her toes. Heat curled into her loins.

For one heart-stopping moment they both froze, too stunned to move. Samantha could feel his eyes on her in the darkness, watching her speculatively. Her breath came short and quick between her suddenly dry lips. Dear God, did he think that she had rolled against him on purpose? Catching back a sob, she scrambled wildly away and hugged the very edge of the mattress.

But the bed seemed no wider than a two-by-four, and the darkness that shrouded them was thick with tension. Samantha lay like a rock, unmoving, the heat from Ross's body lifting the fine hairs at the back of her neck, until she ached from his nearness. She drew in a ragged breath and found herself surrounded by his male scent. Her fingers unconsciously clutched the edge of the mattress as if she were holding on to a life preserver. How could she lie next to him like this all night? she wondered. If she moved nothing more than a finger, she would touch him.

Ignore her, Ross told himself sternly, and get some sleep. He didn't want a woman who would rather sleep on a dirty floor than with him, did he? Forget the feel of her skin, the soft, tempting heat of her. Forget the taste of her on your tongue. And for God's sake, forget that you only have to roll over to have her in your arms!

But his mind was playing tricks on him, and he had only to close his eyes to picture her moving against him, with him, lost in a mindless sea of passion. Sleep was impossible. Seconds stretched into an eternity. Her whispered breathing was a soft call in the night, and his body tightened with need. She was there, in his bed. How could he ignore her when she made him feel like he hadn't had a woman in years? With a muttered curse, he rolled over and reached for her.

Samantha gasped, but it was too late. In one smooth motion he dragged her into his arms and covered her parted lips with his. His tongue was hot, fierce, possessive as it surged into her mouth. He was like a force out of the darkness, sweeping over her before she had a chance to gather her thoughts, scattering her defenses, weakening her with nothing more than the hungry sweep of his tongue and the hard, enticing strength of his body. Heat licked at her, melting her will to fight. She was lost, lost to Raúl's presence in the outer room, lost to who and what this man was. Ross's touch was what she'd feared, what she'd wanted. Thunder rumbled in her veins as the winds of a storm of desire gathered inside her. Her fingers clutched at him as a soft sigh of pleasure rippled through her.

Ross groaned, his arms unconsciously tightening around her slim body, molding her close. The feel of her bare legs entwined with his was sweet torture. He wanted, *needed*, to bury himself in her. But if he took her now, he'd never be able to let her go. He'd never be able to help her escape and leave without him.

His blood cooled at the thought. He'd been sent here to do a job, and nothing could interfere with that. Reluctantly he dragged his mouth from hers, though his arms refused to release her. He needed to hold her just a little longer.

Her breath whispered softly between her parted lips, a moist caress against his mouth, tempting him to forget his scruples and satisfy both of them. But could he ever get enough of her?

His teeth flashed in the darkness. "Ah, Red, you tempt me to take a lot more than a good-night kiss," he whispered in a husky voice that was anything but steady. "But I'm just too tired. So if that's what you've been waiting for, you can relax and go to sleep."

Samantha blinked, his mockery bringing her back to earth with a thud. "Why, you—"

Ross's only response was a lazy chuckle and a familiar pat on her bottom before he released her and turned to stretch out on his stomach with a bone-weary sigh. "'Night, sweetheart."

Her eyes snapped in outrage. "Don't you dare call me 'sweetheart'!" she said. The man was insufferable! How had she ever thought there was a lovable side to him? "If you think I actually *enjoy* your kisses," she ground out between tightly clenched teeth, "you can think again! Why, I'd rather kiss a snake—"

"Raúl's in the next room," Ross mumbled into the pillow. "Be my guest."

A laugh caught her unaware before she hastily swallowed it. Damn him! How could he make her laugh, when she wanted to kill him? And how could he make her want him, when that was the last thing in the world she needed?

With a silent groan she turned and faced the wall, uneasiness roiling in her stomach. She'd never met a man who could make her forget everything but his touch, his loving. Until now. And he was on the wrong side of the law. Dear God, what was she going to do?

She closed her eyes against the sudden sting of tears and clung to the edge of the mattress. Ross's breathing was soft and steady behind her, his body totally relaxed. How could he sleep? she wondered resentfully. Couldn't he hear her heart pounding in the silence? Couldn't he feel the way she ached for him? Did he even care?

She sniffed once or twice, but he lay unmoving, hardening his heart against the need to turn and gather her into his arms. His fingers clenched into a fist. It was better this way, he told himself sternly. Safer. But infinitely less satisfying.

Seconds stretched into minutes, then hours, before exhaustion gradually dragged Samantha into sleep. Her body relaxed and rolled against his, and he, too, finally slept.

Sunrise was a heartbeat away when Ross awoke with a start, his eyes instantly alert in the predawn darkness as he listened for the sound that had awakened him. Silence. It was everywhere, stirred only by the faint whisper of Samantha's breath against his naked chest as she lay cuddled against him in a deep sleep. Sometime during the night she had slipped into his arms, seeking his heat.

Her sweet, feminine scent drifted around him, wooing him, seducing him. His body stirred with need. Gently, so as not to awaken her, his fingers caressed the smooth skin of her back before tangling in the wild beauty of her hair. His eyes trained unseeingly on the ceiling. What was he going to do with her?

He wanted to make love to her. He'd wanted her from the first moment he'd seen her, and nothing had changed. Except that the need had become an ache, the ache a pain that pulled at him even in his sleep. He'd dreamed about her, fantasized about her, and then awoken with her in his arms. She was becoming an obsession, and that scared him.

No one had had a claim on his emotions for a very long time now. In his line of work, an anxious woman interfering at unexpected times was the last thing he needed. So why the hell couldn't he keep his hands off Samantha? He couldn't have her. Not now, not when their very lives depended on him. If Raúl and Manuel began to suspect his emotions were involved, their trust in him would be utterly destroyed.

So where did that leave him? Treating her as if she were his to do with as he willed, a slave to do his bidding and nothing more. She would hate him, despise him, but there wasn't a thing he could do about it, except hold her in the dark and curse the rising of the sun.

The squeak of the screen door was like the clanging of an alarm in the stillness. Ross stiffened. Someone moved about in the outer room on cautious feet. Who the hell was that? Raúl wouldn't be up this early, not after the amount of tequila he had put away last night. Ross had left him sprawled facedown on the couch.

Frowning, Ross gently disentangled himself from the sweetness of Sam's embrace and hurriedly crawled out of bed. She murmured in her sleep, unconsciously moving toward the warmth where he had lain, burrowing under the rough army blanket as Ross pulled it up over her naked shoulders. The urge to touch her one more time had his fingers reaching for her before he realized what he was doing. With a disgusted oath, he grabbed his clothes, instead, and jerked them on, cursing the cold and his own weakness. He pulled on his boots, and without a second glance at the woman who lay sleeping on the bed, he stepped out into the outer room and shut the bedroom door quietly behind him.

At the sight of Manuel trying to waken Raúl, Ross stiffened imperceptibly, the hawklike alertness of his eyes hidden beneath lazy lids. He didn't like Manuel. Raúl was easy to read; more often than not he thought with his loins instead of his brains, which was one of the reasons he wasn't in command. But Manuel was a tricky son of a bitch. Quick-witted and cruel, he was always thinking two steps ahead of the game, always searching for a way to best his opponent. He never played by the rules.

"Where's the *señorita*?" he demanded harshly.

Ross motioned to the door at his back, not liking the look in the other man's eyes. "In bed." He forced a grin that was hard and mocking, concealing the uneasiness that gripped him. "She's a little worse for wear, but she still kicks and scratches whenever she gets the chance. Why? Did you think we'd let her get away?"

"I knew you wouldn't be that stupid," Manuel replied silkily. His thin lips twisted contemptuously when his eyes fell on Raúl and the empty liquor bottle he still clutched in his hand. "I see Raúl didn't sleep alone last night."

"Neither did I," Ross replied softly.

Manuel's black eyes were blank, emotionless, as they silently measured him before he turned to the sink and pumped out a pitcherful of water. Without even glancing at Ross, he carried it over to Raúl's sleeping form and dumped it unceremoniously on his unsuspecting head.

"Ahhh!" Raúl jumped up with an angry sputter, ready to fight, a string of Spanish curses falling off his tongue. He came to a blustering halt at the sight of Manuel. "Manuel! When did you get back?"

"Just now," the other man replied shortly. "Did you sleep well?"

Raúl scowled at his mockery and shot Ross a murderous glance. "Well enough. Did you tell *El Chiso* about our guest? What are we to do with her?"

"Hold her for ransom."

Ross frowned. "How much?"

"Half a million. If we do not receive the money within forty-eight hours, we are to release her in the desert." His smile was tight, cold, cruel. "It is not our fault if she does not survive."

"No!" Raúl protested fiercely. "She is a strong woman. If she makes it through the desert and back across the river, she can identify us."

"She won't make it," Manuel stated flatly.

Ross's gray eyes watched him carefully. "What if she does? She knows where the cabin is."

"Doesn't *El Chiso* realize that?" Raúl asked indignantly. "We can't just let her go!"

"*Fool!*" Manuel snarled scornfully. "Is your brain pickled in tequila? *El Chiso* doesn't care about us! We are peons to him, nothing more. If we're caught, he can always get someone else to do his dirty work for him.''

''So what do we do?'' Raúl countered indignantly. ''Ignore *El Chiso*'s instructions? He is not a man who likes to be crossed.''

Manuel's smile was cunning, feral. ''We have no choice but to protect ourselves. If the ransom doesn't come, we will make sure the *señorita* dies in the desert, and *El Chiso* will be none the wiser.''

A horrified gasp drew all eyes to the bedroom doorway, where Samantha stood, her face devoid of color.

Interlude

Mac all but slammed the receiver back on its hook and just barely resisted the urge to throw the phone across the room. Frustration and fear ate at him like a cancer. Damn them! Did the jackasses in Washington even care that they were all but signing Sam's death warrant?

"Well? What'd they say?"

Mac's tired, worried eyes lifted to Greg Saunders and the other agents who had gathered in his office to wait for news of Sam. Unshaven, exhausted, they had stayed throughout the long hours of the night, pacing restlessly, jumping every time the phone rang. When the call for ransom had finally come through, the relief had been tremendous. She was alive.

But for how long?

"The present administration refuses to negotiate with criminals or terrorists," Mac finally stated flatly. He'd wasted four hours, four precious hours, trying to go by the book. And for what? he thought in disgust. Empty words that didn't accomplish a thing.

"Who cares about their damn policies!" Greg protested, outraged. "What are they going to do? Just sit back and let that scum kill her?"

Bitterness deepened the lines in Mac's weathered face. "The president's putting pressure on the Mexican government to find her. They're doing everything they can." Even to his own ears the words sounded pitifully weak.

L.J. snorted in contempt. "Before or after the *coyotes* kill her?"

Greg's blue eyes narrowed on the clock behind Mac's desk. Time was slipping through their fingers. Panic gripped him as he glared at the older man. "Then to hell with Washington, Mac. We've got to do something! Before it's too late."

"Don't you think I know that?" he growled indignantly. He'd thought of nothing else since L.J. had returned without Sam. His only consolation at this point was that Ross was with her. But not even Ross could single-handedly stop an entire smuggling ring from killing her. "I want that girl back as much as you do."

"We still have almost forty-four hours left," David Martínez reminded them quietly. "What about Sam's family in California? Maybe they could come up with the money."

"A half a million dollars?" L.J. choked. "Man, they don't have that kind of money. Sam's father is dead, and her mother lives off his pension."

"The State Department's been in touch with her mother," Mac added. "She and Sam's three brothers are calling everybody they know, but they'll be lucky if they get fifty thousand. Not many people can put their hands on that kind of cash."

"So what do we do now?" Greg demanded harshly. "Wait for them to dump Sam's body on this side of the river?"

Sam's laughing eyes flashed before Mac, her mischievous grin as clear to him as if she stood before him. "No," he growled roughly, his hazel eyes fierce beneath his bushy brows. He would not sit here and idly twiddle his thumbs while those cutthroats snuffed her out like a candle. He'd tried to follow procedure; now he was going to do things his way. He pushed his chair back sharply from his desk and came to his feet. "Get your chins up off the ground, boys. We've got forty-four hours to get into Mexico and rescue Sam. I'll need some volunteers."

They all clamored to go; he had known they would. He would help out himself if he weren't so old. But he couldn't let any of them go without knowing the chance they were taking.

"You're not going to a barbecue, you know," he told them sternly. "You could get killed if you're not careful. And even if you do make it back alive, you're laying your job on the line if this blows up in our faces and Washington finds out about it."

"I don't care," L.J. replied, his face grim. "I was the last one to see Sam. I'm the only one who knows where to start looking for her. I'm going."

"You'll need a good tracker," David Martínez added, his dark eyes locking with Mac's. "And I'm the best one you've got. With L.J. showing me where to start, I'll find her."

Mac nodded, satisfied. "Just get in and out as quick as you can. And avoid bloodshed if it's at all possible. We don't want to draw any more attention to this than we have to."

"We'll be back before you know it," L.J. told him confidently.

Mac sighed and reached for the phone. "I hope so. But I'm going to keep trying to talk some sense into those morons in Washington and see about raising the ransom money somehow. I hope to God we won't need it."

Chapter Six

Time was running out. Samantha stood in the shade of an old pine tree that grew near the northeast corner of the house and stared at the distant horizon. A cool wind raced up the side of the mountain to play with her hair, lifting the coppery tendrils at her temples. Freedom. It was there in the distance, across the flat expanse of the desert, wavering before her eyes like a mirage. And it was as elusive as the desert sand that ran before the wind.

A shiver slid down her spine, and she hugged herself, her fingers unconsciously biting into her arms. Her eyes never left the horizon. How much time did she have? she wondered, fighting the panic that pulled at her. Thirty-six hours? Less? And what difference did it make, anyway? There would be no ransom money.

Silently she admitted that fact to herself, accepting the inevitable without bitterness. The visions of her family that danced before her eyes brought the hot thickness of tears to her throat as nothing else could have. Her mother, with her patient smile, and the three brothers who had seen that she never lacked for a father figure. Jack, who had taught her to love sports; Tommy, with a grin as big as Texas; and Mark, the eldest, who still tried to protect them all. Even now they would be grieving for her, hurting, and desperately trying to come up with the cash to save her. They couldn't get it—they didn't have it—but they'd try, anyway. And when time ran out, they'd always blame themselves for not doing enough to save her.

Her teeth clenched on a violent oath. Damn the smugglers! She would not let them do that to her family, to her. Somehow she would find a way to get out of this.

Through narrowed eyes she studied the contour of the land, and knew she could make it. The house and outbuildings were concealed in pines at the top of a ridge. On one side the terrain dropped steeply down to the desert, while the other three sides merged into the mountain. Boulders, some as large as the house, looked as if they had been tossed about the landscape with a careless hand. They would offer easy concealment, especially in the dark, and make tracking by horseback slow and difficult.

But first she had to get away from her captors.

She didn't have to look over her shoulder to know that she was under constant surveillance. They had given her the freedom of the house and yard, but she was never alone. She felt the touch of their eyes at unexpected moments, the bitter taste of fear on her tongue whenever Raúl or Manuel came too close, the skidding of her heart whenever she looked up and found Ross watching her.

Her fingers curled into her palms. He was avoiding her. Ever since this morning when she'd unexpectedly learned of their plans for her, he'd kept his distance. His face was closed to all expression; his gray eyes were wintry as he'd watched her from beneath hooded lids. He wasn't going to help her.

A hurt she refused to acknowledge twisted in her like a snake. Did he think she would turn to him just because he had stirred her with a few stolen kisses in the dark? She expected nothing from him, *nothing*.

From the shadow of the barn, Ross ground out a cigarette with his heel as he watched her huddle against the house, her troubled eyes trained northward. She appeared small and vulnerable in the white shirt he had loaned her. It came down to her knees, swallowing her and somehow making her look incredibly sexy. His body stirred, and without quite realizing it, he found himself walking toward her, unable to stay away.

A self-deprecating smile curved his mouth. You've got it bad, man, a small voice jeered in his head. What the hell are you going to do now?

Save her.

He'd known from the beginning he would have to blow his cover for her. He'd struggled against it, resisted it and lost. He laughed harshly, without humor. A woman, for God's sakes! For the first time in his career he was blowing his cover for a woman. And he was so close to discovering *El Chiso*'s identity. A week—two weeks, tops—and he'd have everything he needed to shut down the smuggling ring for good. Now that was out of the question.

Time was running out.

She was obviously looking for a way out. He watched her eyes scan the horizon, and found himself wanting to drag her into his arms, to kiss her into mindlessness. What he wouldn't give to have her to himself just for an hour! An hour without fear, without a thought to the ticking of the clock, without her struggling against her attraction to him because of who she thought he was. And he'd have it, by God, when he got her out of here! Until then, they both had to be patient.

A twig snapped under his booted foot as he came up behind her. When her eyes flew to his in alarm, he leaned against the pine tree and crossed his arms across his chest, his shoulder just inches away from hers. "Planning on making a break for it?" he asked softly.

She lifted her chin, her blue eyes sparkling defiantly. "The idea has crossed my mind," she admitted boldly. "After all, what do I have to lose?"

"Your life, for one thing," he growled roughly, angered by her bravado. Damn her, she was going to do something stupid! "You're not giving your family much credit. If they come through with the ransom..."

"They won't," she cut in flatly. "They can't." Her gaze strayed back to the northern horizon. "They couldn't come up with that kind of money if they sold everything they had. They're rich in a lot of things, but money isn't one of them."

So there would be no help from that quarter. His jaw clenched as an unfamiliar feeling of helplessness caught him off guard. Anger rippled through him. What was she doing in this mess, anyway? he fumed. She had people who loved her, worried about her!

He glared at her, his eyes hostile. "What kind of woman are you?" he demanded irritably. "You've got people who care about you, but I bet you didn't give them a thought when you set up that surveillance at the river. You didn't, did you?" he pressed. He saw the guilt flicker in her eyes, and reached out to grab her shoulders. "Damn it, why aren't you back in Presidio, changing diapers and fixing school lunches for a handful of kids? Why aren't you married?"

"Because I'm not Suzy Homemaker," she snapped, stung by his criticism. "Getting married isn't every woman's goal in life." She jerked free of his touch and stabbed him in the chest with her finger. "What about you?" she countered, turning the tables on him. "Did you think about your family before you went into this line of work? Why don't you have a wife and kids and a station wagon? Why aren't you married?"

Because he'd never wanted that. Until now. The realization hit him like a ton of bricks. He wanted out of the shadows; he had for a long time now. But a wife? And kids? Was he ready for that?

A sudden picture of blue-eyed little girls with waves of fiery curls tumbling around mischievous faces exploded before his mind's eye. They would be a handful—independent, adventuresome, delightful—just like Samantha. What a wild and unconventional mother she would be.

And the man who gave her those children? Resentment flared at the thought of anyone else touching her, having her. She was his, and when all this was over he was going to prove it.

"Maybe I never found a woman who could make me want those things, Red," he said quietly. "And maybe you never found the right man. Have you ever stopped to consider that?"

Samantha stared at him in surprise, her eyes searching his, the dull pounding of her heart echoing softly in her ears. "I wouldn't have thought you were a man for what-ifs."

A grin tugged at his lips. "Maybe I'm mellowing in my old age. Or maybe you're the woman I've been looking for all these years." He watched stunned surprise tumble into her eyes. "Think about it."

She didn't want to think about it! She already knew what it was like to lose herself in his arms, and he had done nothing more than kiss her. What would it be like if they had met under different circumstances?

Heat surged into her cheeks. "I don't have to think about it," she replied stiffly. "I don't have time for what-ifs."

The humor fled from Ross's eyes as they snared hers. "You don't know what destiny has in store for you, Red. Don't do anything stupid."

"I'm not going to sit around and wait to die."

No, she wouldn't. She would fight to the bitter end, knowing the odds were against her, knowing she had no one to depend on but herself. In her place he'd have done the same thing.

But she wasn't really alone. Could he trust her enough to tell her? He studied her searchingly, noting the dark shadows under her eyes, the paleness of her cheeks, the desperation that curled her fingers into fists. She was not a woman good at hiding her feelings. How could he tell her that he worked on the same side of the law as she? Raúl and Manuel would only have to look at her face to know that something was up.

He swore softly. "Just don't run off half-cocked," he said tightly. "Manuel would take great pleasure in using you for target practice." And before she could say another word, he turned and strode toward the barn.

Samantha bit her lip to stop from calling out after him, confusion clouding her eyes. Would she ever understand him? Would she have the time? He was one of them, a smuggler, yet she was sure she hadn't misunderstood his subtle message. He was warning her. But why? What did he know that she didn't?

The answers evaded her, and as the afternoon wore on, she couldn't think of anything but the slow, ceaseless passage of time. Slowly, imperceptibly, a noose was tightening around her neck and there was nothing she could do to stop it. She'd never felt so helpless in her life.

Ironically, she welcomed the coming of evening. From the porch steps she watched the sun dip behind the mountains, leaving violet clouds to feather the horizon. One by one the stars appeared in the cold, darkening sky. Without the heat of the sun, the air quickly turned chilly, and shivering, Samantha rose to go inside. For an hour or two, she could immerse herself in the mundane chores of cooking and try to pretend that time stood still. She wasn't fooling anyone, least of all herself, but it helped her hang on to her sanity.

When she stepped into the kitchen, she found herself unconsciously looking for Ross. Every time she'd come near the stove today, he'd suddenly appeared at her side. Breakfast would have been a disaster without his help.

She winced, her face drawn, as visions of the morning passed before her eyes. The news that they really did intend to kill her had left her shaking. Somehow she'd never expected them to go that far. She'd been lost, dazed, when Ross hustled her over to the stove and ordered her to make biscuits. She'd looked at him as though he'd lost his mind, and in the end he was the one who baked the bread.

By lunchtime, she'd felt better, and hadn't really needed his help. Leftover biscuits and canned beans weren't all that difficult, but he'd insisted. He'd already tasted her beans and said he preferred his own. She suspected he'd been afraid she would burn herself on the stove.

The screen door banged behind her, jerking her out of her musings. She whirled and automatically stepped back as Raúl came toward her. From the corner of her eye, she saw Manuel take a seat on the couch, his blank eyes watching her, always watching her.

"Here's the meat for supper, *señorita*," Raúl said with a cruel grin. "Try not to burn it, okay?" He tossed it carelessly into the sink.

Samantha stared down at the bloody, skinless carcasses and felt the blood drain from her face. She couldn't seem to tear her eyes away. "What is it?" she whispered hoarsely.

"Rabbit."

Samantha swayed. The sight of blood had always sickened her. Over the years she'd tried to overcome the weakness, hating the thought of being a faint-hearted female, and up to a point she had succeeded. But Raúl had caught her off guard. She hadn't had the chance to steel herself against the nausea. Her hand went to her throat, her fingers fluttering helplessly. "I can't cook that," she choked.

His black eyes narrowed dangerously. "We will get the ransom money whether you are dead or alive, *señorita*. Don't push your luck."

He wanted her to defy him—she could see it in his eyes. He'd been watching her all day, laughing at the distress she hadn't been able to conceal, biding his time. He'd like nothing more than to shoot her just as he had those poor little rabbits. And Manuel wouldn't lift a finger to stop him.

She stiffened. They were going to kill her if she didn't find a way to escape. There was nothing she could do to stop them, but she'd be damned if they'd get any satisfaction out of it. Her eyes had a chilled expression as they met Raúl's. "How do you want it cooked?"

"Fried."

She nodded and turned back to the sink. For what seemed an eternity, she felt his presence at her back, his hot breath at her neck making her skin crawl. Fear lodged somewhere in her throat.

When she heard the springs of the couch groan with his weight as he took a seat next to Manuel, she closed her eyes weakly and let the air out of her lungs in a silent, ragged rush. She hadn't even realized she was holding her breath. With trembling fingers she searched in the drawer next to the stove for a knife, her eyes deliberately avoiding the contents of the sink.

Cut it up and fry it, she told herself fiercely. And don't think about it. You can do it.

But in the end she couldn't. Her fingers clutching an old paring knife, she turned to the sink and let her eyes drop to the skinless rabbits. Bile rose in her throat. The knife dropped to the floor with a clatter, but she never even noticed. She had to get out of here before she made a fool of herself in front of these men! She whirled, her eyes desperate in a face the color of parchment, and ran for the door.

Raúl jumped up to grab her, only to stop short at the sight of her green face. He laughed mockingly. "Where are you running off to, *señorita*? You have some rabbits to cook."

Samantha only groaned and pushed past him, the echo of his and Manuel's laughter ringing in her ears.

She ran out into the night, stumbling off the porch and into the darkness, her face ashen as she leaned weakly against the side of the house and lost the contents of her stomach.

Damn them. Damn them all! she silently raged, catching back a sob as hot tears stung her eyes. What kind of animals were they? They took malicious delight in taunting her, in bringing her to her knees. They would kill her with equal relish and laugh while they did it. Dear God, she had to get out of here!

"Are you all right?"

She cried out in alarm as Ross suddenly materialized out of the darkness. He stood just inches from her, the light that spilled from the house at his back, casting his face in shadows. The quiet concern she'd heard in his voice was almost her undoing. She forced her shoulders to straighten. "Of course I'm all right," she said tightly. "I'm on top of the world."

Her sarcasm rolled off him like water off a duck's back. He'd seen Raúl return with the skinned rabbits, and from a shadowed corner of the porch, he'd watched her desperate figure emerge from the house. He'd told himself to let her be, to let her work this out in her own way, to keep his distance just as he had for most of the day so Manuel and Raúl would never suspect his emotions were involved. But the battle had been lost before it even began, and he'd gone to her.

He reached for her. "Come here." And before she could even gasp in protest, he gently wiped her hot face with a handkerchief he had pulled out of his pocket and had dampened at the pump. He watched her eyes close on a sigh and felt a sweet rush of tenderness slide into his stomach. His arm slipped around her shoulders to pull her close. "How's that?" he asked huskily as he caressed her face once again with the cool handkerchief. "Better?"

Samantha gazed at him helplessly, tears welling in her eyes. Oh, God, don't be nice to me, she prayed silently. Not again, not when she was desperate, alone, racing with the clock for her very life. She wanted to hate him the way she did Raúl and Manuel, to despise him and turn cold at his touch. Instead she fell apart at a simple act of kindness.

Didn't he know she was too vulnerable now? She could fight his mockery, his arrogance, but his sympathy, his unexpected show of tenderness, left her helpless in his arms. She wanted, *needed*, to read so much more into his action than there was. That more than anything terrified her.

She'd never needed a man before.

His taste was something she could become addicted to, his strength something she could grow to lean on. He made her forget that they were enemies, that he was just as responsible for her presence here as the others. How could she let him do that to her? How could she let herself need him? He jerked her emotions around like a yo-yo on a string. One minute he was a cold, unfeeling kidnapper, the next a warm, sensual seducer who could melt her bones like hot butter. Where was her pride?

She jerked free of his touch to glare at him, her fingers balled into fists. "Better?" she challenged, her eyes snapping. "Do you think your touching show of sympathy is going to make it *better*? It's only a matter of hours before you and your friends kill me. If you really want to make me feel better, do something about that!''

She stormed into the house without waiting for his response, color flying high in her cheeks, her jaw clenched tight with resolve as the screen door slammed loudly behind her. When Raúl taunted her about her queasiness, she withered him with a glance and returned to the sink. The knife was still on the floor where she'd dropped it.

Her movements were automatic as she picked it up and rinsed it off. Possibilities ricocheted in her head. She reached for the rabbits, closing her mind to what she was doing as she began to cut them into pieces suitable for frying. Her eyes lingered on the knife, as her fingers clutched it. It wasn't much to look at. Old and rusty, it had been sharpened so many times that the blade was thin and worn. But it was the only weapon she had. Tonight, she promised herself. Tonight she was getting out of here.

Hope stirred in her heart, and for the first time since she'd learned of the ransom request, she felt she had a chance. Granted, it was a pitiful one at best, but it was the only one she was likely to get. And she'd never been one to look a gift horse in the mouth. All she had to do now was get through supper without letting anyone guess her intentions.

That proved to be easier than she'd expected. Despite the fact that she'd cleaned the meat and dredged it with flour, the sight of it still turned her stomach and left her eyes wide and distressed in her pale face. On more than one occasion, she thought she was going to have to run back outside. Only Raúl's taunting gibes kept her stubbornly at the stove.

She managed to cook the meat without burning it, though later she never knew how. Escape! The thought ran through her head like a refrain, urging her to slip the knife into the pocket of her slacks when no one was looking, tempting her to take some food. She eyed the hard biscuits that were left from lunch and reluctantly discarded the idea. The presence of the knife in her pocket was infinitely reassuring. The knife would be enough. Food would be too hard to conceal.

She made herself eat supper. With each bite she choked down, she thought of the miles she would make before dawn. Swallowing became easier. Until she looked up and found her eyes trapped by Ross's gray ones.

He knew what she was up to. Would he stop her?

Silently they measured each other from across the room. The dull pounding of her heart was like a distant echo in Samantha's ears. Vaguely she wondered if Ross could hear it. His face was grim, his eyes intense. Unconsciously her gaze lingered on his mouth. Memories stirred, heating her. She had seen his mouth relaxed in laughter, sweet with tenderness, sensuous and possessive in passion. He could make her weak, make her ache. And after tonight she would never see him again. Except in her dreams. Somehow she knew he would always be in her dreams.

Blindly her eyes dropped to her plate as an unbearable emptiness spread inside her chest like a cold fog. Her heart constricted with a pain that was unlike anything she had ever felt before. Don't, she told herself sternly, blinking back tears. Don't cry for something that was impossible from the very beginning. When the time came, she was going to turn her back on him and walk away. No, she was going to run. Maybe then it wouldn't hurt so badly.

With fingers that shook only slightly, she reached for another bite of rabbit.

Her resolves, however, were not so firm when it came time for bed. They all seemed to be waiting for something to happen. Manuel didn't question Ross's right to have her in his bed, but his unblinking eyes were unnerving as he watched them go into the other room. Samantha was shaking when Ross shut the door, enclosing them in darkness.

Ross leaned against the door, his eyes trained on where he knew she stood. "Why don't you light the candle," he suggested softly.

She stiffened as his voice swept up her back like a warm caress, but she did as he requested. Or at least, she tried. Her fingers were all thumbs, crumbling two of the cardboard matches without even producing a spark. With a muttered oath she blindly searched for a third.

Ross's strong fingers closed around hers. "Here, let me," he said, laughing. "You seem to be having a problem."

The match flared, and the flame reflected in his eyes as he cupped his hand around it and bent to light the wick of the candle. Samantha stood only inches from him, mesmerized, wondering not for the first time what he would look like without the beard and long hair. Would she pass him on the street and not know him? Her heart knocked against her ribs. No, never. She would know the arrogant tilt of his chin and the flashing devilment of his grin anywhere.

She watched his mouth twitch, and suddenly realized she was staring. Her eyes flew to his. He winked. "Ready for bed?"

"No!" she groaned, and whirled. Her gaze fell on the bed. Panic knotted her stomach. She couldn't get into that bed with him standing there watching her. "I ... I'm not really tired."

"Well, that's too bad, because I am." His fingers moved to the buttons of his shirt. When she stood there, unmoving, he frowned. "Are you going to stand there all night? Hurry up and get undressed."

Undressed? No! She was going to sleep in her clothes and slip away just as soon as everyone was asleep. If she had to dress again, she was bound to awaken him. "I'll sleep in my clothes," she said faintly. "I ... I got cold last night."

"No."

Samantha stopped halfway to the bed. "What do you mean no?" she demanded indignantly, whirling to face him. "I don't have to ask your permission to sleep in my clothes."

"Think again, Red," he said quietly. "We're going to do this just the way we did last night. Now are you going to come out of those clothes, or do you want me to help you?"

He was serious! Unconsciously Samantha's fingers went to the knife in her pocket. Damn him! He had no reason to expect her to strip and climb into bed with him as if they were old, familiar lovers! "Ross, for God's sake—"

He stepped toward her purposefully, his eyes alight with a fire that set her pulses pounding. "You haven't got anything I haven't seen before, but if this is the way you want it..."

"No, damn you, you win!" Her eyes shot daggers at him as she pulled off her boots and her fingers reached for the fastening of her slacks. She dropped them to the floor without ever releasing his gaze. Her shirt soon followed suit. "Is this enough?" she asked bitterly, standing stiffly before him in nothing but her bra and panties. She lifted her chin defiantly, cursing the fire that burned her cheeks. "Or do you want me completely naked?"

"Don't ask me what I want, Sam," he rasped thickly. "Not unless you're ready to hear my answer. Get into bed."

She did as he commanded, but with a cool superiority he couldn't help but admire. His hungry eyes roamed the straight line of her back, the small waist he could easily span with his hands, the gentle flare of her hips. The fire in his blood turned into a blaze.

He extinguished the candle with a terse blow and let his own clothes fall to the floor. When he slid into bed, she silently, coldly, presented him with her back.

Frustration whipped at him. She had no one to blame for this but herself. He couldn't take the chance that he'd be asleep when she tried to steal out of there in the middle of the night. And he knew she would make her move tonight. He'd have done the same thing. They were a lot alike; so much alike it stunned him at times.

But where he was hard, she was soft. The remembered feel of her skin under his fingers suddenly tugged at his senses. Satin. She was like satin, he realized with an ache. And hot to the touch. Didn't she know he couldn't lie with her this way and not touch her? He couldn't stop himself. His fingers reached for her.

Samantha stiffened at the feel of his hand on her arm. No! she wanted to cry. She didn't want the gentleness that he let out under the cover of darkness. It would only make her leaving that much more difficult.

But the pounding of her heart told her she did want it.

His fingers moved from her arm to her shoulder to the curve of her hip, wooing her with a caress that was as soft and fleeting as a whisper in the night. She clamped her teeth on a sigh, steeling herself to ignore the pleasure. But it seeped into her bones, and with each passing second the struggle became fiercer, the outcome less certain. How much more of this could she take before she turned to him?

Ross stared at her stiff back, his body on fire, the feel of her feeding the flames that licked at him. She wasn't fooling him for a second. The fire that raged in him burned inside her, too. But she'd be damned if she'd give him the satisfaction of an honest response.

It hurt, he realized suddenly. With an angry curse he snatched his hand away as if he'd been burned and rolled to his back. Damn her! When had he given her the power to hurt him?

Coldness invaded the bed. He wouldn't touch her again, and they both knew it. Samantha blinked back tears and told herself this was what she wanted. She wanted no regrets when she left here, no what-ifs. She couldn't live with that!

So they lay still, like two strangers suddenly caught in an intimate position, afraid to move, afraid to trust. Each passing second was an eternity without end, torture at its finest. Hours passed before she finally heard his breathing ease into sleep. Even then, the need to turn to him was almost her undoing. But she realized she didn't need the memory of watching him sleep.

From the outer room, she heard Raúl's steady snoring and Manuel's wheezy breathing. How long since they had gone to sleep? she wondered with a frown. She would wait another hour, maybe two.

But time dragged, and she almost nodded off, only to jerk herself awake again. Her heart skidded in alarm. If she fell asleep, she'd lose any chance she had of escaping. She had to try now, before it was too late.

Slowly, hardly daring to breathe, she turned to face Ross. In the darkness, she could see he lay on his back, one arm shielding his eyes. With a quiet touch she pushed the blanket aside, freeing her legs. The thundering of her heart was loud in her ears. Surely he could hear it!

But he never moved.

Her nerves tightened as she tensed to climb over him. He was so big and the bed was so small it was almost impossible to move over him without touching him. The night air was cold against her bare skin as she swung her leg over him, but she ignored the discomfort. Her eyes locked on his sleeping face as her foot searched for the floor. The sigh that had welled up in her almost escaped as she finally found it. With a slowness that had her muscles screaming in protest, she eased the rest of her body over him and came to her feet.

He never moved.

She found it impossible to drag her eyes away from him even to search for her clothes. She found them blindly and pulled them on, her movements amplified in her own ears though she knew she'd been extremely quiet. The zipper on her pants was ignored. She'd carry her shoes until she got outside.

She started for the door and hesitated. Ross. Silently she said his name. The pain that had gathered in her closed around her heart like a fist. How could she leave him? How could she not? Circumstances had thrown them together, and circumstances were tearing them apart. But not before she'd lost her heart to him, she realized with a sob. Of all the men she could have fallen for, why did fate have to pick Ross de la Garza for her? He was a man she couldn't have!

Pain raced through her. Get out! her heart cried. Now! She reached for the door handle.

Suddenly, from out of the darkness, long, lean fingers clamped around her wrist like a vice. "What the *hell* do you think you're doing?"

Chapter Seven

Ross's whisper was low and fierce, an angry demand that was all the more dangerous for its silky softness. Samantha gasped, fear clutching her heart. He'd caught her red-handed.

No! she wanted to scream, tugging at his hold on her. She wouldn't let it end this way. Not when freedom was just on the other side of that door and she could all but smell it. All he had to do was let her go, let her slip outside and out of his life forever. No one would ever have to know she hadn't escaped while he was asleep. Was that asking too much?

From Ross de la Garza? Yes.

Anger, sharp and clean as a scalpel, sliced through her. Damn him! He'd been waging a silent war with her ever since they'd met, pitting his strength, his cunning, against hers time after time after time. He wouldn't *let* her win, any more than she would let him decide her fate for her. She was escaping. Tonight. If he thought he could stop her, let him try.

She jerked at her arm, but when his fingers only tightened, her temper exploded. "Let go of me!" she demanded. Her nails raced for his face.

She fought like someone who had nothing to lose, no holds barred, the struggle silent and furious in the dark. Ross fended her off, dodging her blows, only to wince as her nails ripped at his naked chest. His teeth clamped down on a scathing curse. Little wildcat! He'd like to shake her until her teeth rattled. She thought she was so smart! If he let her, she'd waltz right out that door and try to make it on her own. She'd never even make it out of the house.

She should have asked him for help, he fumed, knowing he was being unreasonable but unable to stop himself. His blood ran cold at the thought of her at the mercy of Raúl or Manuel.

"Calm down, you little witch!" he muttered, taking care to keep his voice below a whisper when her bare foot came down on his. With a silent curse, he found her wrists in the darkness and dragged them behind her back, forcing her against him until her face was buried in his chest. The softness of her thighs scorched his. Could he ever touch her without wanting her? "I ought to beat some sense into you!"

"No!" she choked against his bare shoulder, gasping for breath. "Let me go!"

"Why?" he demanded, his breath hot against her ear. He frowned at the sound of her tear-laced voice.

Did she have any idea what her tears did to him? He felt himself weaken, his arms suddenly gentle, cradled her, and stiffened. "So you can open that door and get yourself killed?"

"I would have made it."

"Like hell!" he whispered, almost shaking her. "Listen. Manuel is sleeping right outside the door." The echo of the smuggler's ragged breathing carried easily in the silence. The sound obviously came from right outside. When Samantha's eyes widened in alarm, Ross couldn't stop himself from pulling her closer. "If you really want to escape, try the window. It's safer."

The window? She blinked in confusion, her stunned eyes lifting to his. In disbelief, she watched a crooked grin slowly stretch across his face. He was going to help her. He was actually going to help her! She clutched at him. "Ross, why—"

"We'll discuss it later," he said softly, cutting her off as he urged her toward the patch of moonlight that spilled through the window. "First we've got to get out of here."

"But the window's nailed shut."

"Only at the bottom," he replied with a quick smile. "We'll lower the top sash."

Samantha turned to gaze at the window. The light from the moon clearly revealed that he was right. Why hadn't she thought to look at the top pane? "I should have seen that," she muttered, glancing back over her shoulder at him. "But I didn't even look—"

The words died in her throat. He stood behind her, pulling on his clothes. Warmth spread into Samantha's stomach at the sight of him. The moonlight slid over him like the hands of a lover, dancing in the dark thickness of his hair and beard. His face was cast in shadows, rugged, sensuous. He moved with the easy grace of a man who knew exactly what he was doing, where he was going, and Samantha could have watched him for hours.

When he looked up and caught her eyes on him, he smiled. There were promises in that smile, and an emotion she couldn't put a name to. All the doubts, all the barriers that had helped her keep him at arm's length, shattered. She realized suddenly that whoever he was, *whatever* he was, there was no longer any need to run from him. Had there ever been? Hadn't she always been afraid of what he could make her feel rather than the physical harm he might do her?

Her heart rocked at its mooring as need rolled into her, swift, hot and sweet. She knew he could read the emotions in her eyes, but she didn't look away. She couldn't.

Ross's eyes burned into hers as he tucked his shirt into his jeans and walked toward her on silent feet. Something had changed between them, an indescribable something that had the very air humming between them. She was different.

Trusting.

The word hit him like a bouquet of colorful balloons. He wanted to laugh, to hug her, to never let her go. What had he ever done to deserve her? She gave him her trust so easily, without question, without reservations. And for all she knew, he was still a smuggler, an outlaw. Yet she trusted him.

His fingers slid over her cheek in wonder, once again marveling at the softness of her skin. If he lived to be a hundred, he would never tire of touching her. "Ready?" he asked huskily.

"For anything," she admitted softly.

The need to take her into his arms had never been so strong. But there wasn't time! He turned toward the window and motioned for her silence. He didn't have to tell her that one false move now would mean the end of them. He could tell she realized this by the fear reflected in her eyes.

He reached for the upper windowpane, his fingers silently gripping each side of the framework. With infinite patience, he lowered the window a fraction, unconsciously holding his breath as he waited for the old wood to groan in resistance. But it only emitted a sigh that was drowned out by the snoring in the other room.

Exhilaration shot through him. It was going to work!

Samantha bit her bottom lip to stop herself from rushing him as she watched him lower the window with painstaking slowness. The cold night air swept in with the moonlight, and she could almost feel time slipping through her fingers. Her eyes went to the closed bedroom door before swinging back to the window. Her nails cut into her palms as she watched the concentration that turned Ross's beard-shadowed jaw to granite. A few more inches and they would be able to squeeze through.

The window shuddered.

The sound was like a rifle shot in the darkness. Ross froze instantly, his blood running cold, his eyes on Samantha's suddenly ashen face. For what seemed like an eternity, they held their breaths and waited. Any second now the door would burst open.

But nobody stirred.

Ross released his breath in a slow, almost soundless sigh and reached for Sam. She came to him willingly. "We're not taking any more chances," he breathed into her ear as his arms slid around her. "Think you can squeeze through?"

Her eyes lifted to the two-foot opening. "Yes," she whispered huskily, trying to ignore the way his breath stirred her blood. "But what about you? It looks awfully small . . ."

"Don't worry about me," he assured her. "I've gotten through a lot tighter spots than this." He motioned to the thin ledge that formed the sill. "Step up here and swing your leg over the frame. And whatever you do, don't kick the glass. It's so old and brittle, it'd probably shatter if you touched it. Once you jump free, I'll throw both pairs of our boots out to you. Okay?"

She nodded and took a steadying breath before she moved to step up on the sill.

Ross stopped her before she'd even lifted her foot. At her look of surprise, he smiled and pulled her back against him. "For luck," he murmured, and covered her mouth with his.

It was a kiss unlike any he had ever given her. Sweet, possessive, hungry, and tender with unspoken promises. Samantha melted against him, her arms crawling up around the strong column of his neck as her bones slowly liquified. Heat poured through her at the flick of his tongue teasing hers.

Her moan of pleasure was soft against his mouth. The taste of her went straight to his head, and desire flowed thick and heavy in his veins. A few more minutes, he promised himself fiercely. She was so sweet, so willing. And she was running for her life. He groaned, his arms tightening around her convulsively before he slowly, reluctantly pushed her away. At the sight of the passion shining in her sapphire eyes, he cursed the fates and urged her toward the window. "Come on," he rasped. "Let's get out of here."

And before she knew it, she found herself perched in the open window, Ross's hands at her hips, balancing her, freedom just a jump away. Her heart thundered in her breast as she hesitated, her gaze swinging back over her shoulder to find him in the moonlight. "Why are you doing this?" she asked suddenly in a hushed whisper. "Why are you risking your life to help me?"

His grin was quick, wicked, unrepentant. "Because I'm on the same side you are," he admitted in a voice laced with laughter. "Mac would skin me alive if I let anything happen to you." The hands at her hips gave a gentle nudge. "Out you go, sweetheart."

Mac!

Samantha's stocking feet hit the hard ground with a soft thud, her knees automatically bending to break the shock of the fall, her thoughts tumbling around in confusion. How did he know Mac? Just who was Ross de la Garza?

She stared up at the window, frowning at the suspicions that swirled in her mind, but he gave her little time to think. Her boots were tossed down to her, then his. In the next instant he was beside her, his gray eyes sharp and intense as he grabbed her hand and pulled her to the trees at the edge of the yard, taking care to avoid the glaring brightness of the moonlight.

This man was a professional, Samantha realized suddenly. It showed up in every move he made. The caution, the hardness, the eyes that never missed a trick, the confidence that was such an essential part of him. Why hadn't she seen it before? He wasn't the type who would waste his talents as a henchman in a smuggling ring. He'd be the leader.

"Who are you?" she demanded hoarsely. "How do you know Mac?"

Ross stopped at the edge of the trees, his hand still holding hers as he gauged the distance from the concealing shadows where they stood, to the shed and connecting corral, where the horses were kept. Fifty yards of moonlight. "I've known Mac since I was a kid," he answered absently, his keen gaze sweeping to the ramshackle outbuilding where the aliens slept before coming back to the shed. "I've been working undercover for him for the past two months." He turned to her without warning, his eyes a steel trap that captured hers with ease. "We've got to get to the shed and get a horse. And that moonlight's going to pick us up like a spotlight. We'll have to run for it. Ready?"

She nodded, her voice deserting her, her fingers unconsciously clinging to his. He gave her hand a squeeze of encouragement, then took off, pulling her after him.

He was an agent. The thought tumbled in her head even as she raced after him, her feet flying over the ground as she tried to keep up with him. She'd never been alone. He'd been there right from the beginning. Protecting her, watching over her. And he'd never said a word.

She frowned, images flashing before her mind's eye in quick succession. He'd seen her scared, terrified, crying, desperate. He hadn't once tried to reassure her with the knowledge of who he was. She swallowed a bitter laugh as hurt clouded her eyes. Reassure her, ha! He'd taken every opportunity to infuriate her. How could he have treated her so callously?

The protective darkness of the shed suddenly enveloped them, the smell of hay and horses blocking out the sweet freshness of the night. Samantha jerked her hand free and practically threw his boots at him. "You're despicable!" she hissed, her breasts heaving with outrage as she glared at his shadowy face. He wasn't even winded. "You unfeeling bastard! You knew I was terrified. Why didn't you say something?"

He'd known she would react this way, but he wasn't a man who often had to explain his actions. "I couldn't take the chance that you'd give me away," he said stiffly, his face turning to granite before her very eyes. He tugged on his boots and turned toward the horses, finding his way unerringly in the darkness. "Do you think we could save this discussion for later?

I don't know about you, but I'd like to get out of here before our friends in the house realize we're gone.''

He was right, of course, she thought in disgust. But later she would tell him exactly how she felt about him! "What do you want me to do?" she asked coolly, swiftly pulling on her own boots.

"Bring me the bridle hanging on that post," he commanded as he threw first a horse blanket and then the saddle on his black mare. He tightened the cinch, his movements quick and sure, his gaze constantly shifting to the open doorway of the shed. He could see the house sitting in the moonlight. Nothing moved.

The other horses in the corral shifted restlessly. Ross turned sharply, drawing an almost soundless gasp from Sam. Her heart pounded, the sudden coppery taste of fear bitter in her mouth, pushing away the anger that had gripped her only seconds before. The concealing darkness of the shed was suddenly threatening. "Ross?"

The alarm in her voice had him reaching for her. His fingers closed over hers reassuringly. "It's okay. It's just the horses."

But his eyes were as sharp and wary as a cornered mountain lion's as he scanned the darkness. Someone was out there. He could feel it, smell it. His nostrils flared at the scent of danger. Once, years ago, he'd walked down a dark alley in Teheran and smelled that same odor, felt that same prickling of his skin as someone watched him from the darkness. He'd been lucky to make it out of that alley alive.

Suddenly that sixth sense that had always come to his rescue warned him there wasn't time to saddle another horse. He pulled Sam after him as he tugged the mare toward the open end of the shed that faced away from the house. He stopped in the shadowy doorway. "Time to mount up—"

The click of a gun being cocked ripped through the darkness.

One minute they stood as if turned to stone, and the next Ross was moving like lightning, jerking Sam behind the mare before she even realized what was happening. He felt the exact moment fear grabbed her, but could do nothing to reassure her. What could he say? His gun was hanging on the gun rack just inside the front door of the cabin.

The silence that gripped the night was cold, wicked, deadly. The training that had served Ross well in the past fell into place like an old, comfortable coat. His face grim, his eyes sharp and cold, he scanned the dark shadows just beyond the stretch of moonlight that spilled into the wide doorway, but the blackness was inky, cryptic. At the other end of the shed was more moonlight. There was no question of slipping out under cover of darkness.

"Step out from behind the horse," a voice suddenly ordered curtly from the direction of the trees. *"Slowly."*

Samantha's eyes widened in shock. "L.J.!" she breathed softly. He hadn't left her to get of this mess alone. He'd come back for her. "Ross, it's L.J.!" Tears of relief bubbled in her as she stepped toward the shadows, searching for him in the darkness. "L.J., I'm okay! Where are you?"

Ross cursed fiercely and reached for her, alarm racing through him as she unwittingly moved into the moonlight. Had she lost her mind? If Manuel or Raúl woke up and looked out the window, she'd be dead meat. "Damn it to hell, woman, get back in the shadows!"

"Let her go," L.J. growled harshly. "Now. Before I shoot you right between the eyes like you deserve!"

Moonlight glittered on the barrel of a rifle pointed right at Ross's chest. Samantha's eyes widened in horror. L.J. didn't know! She stepped closer to the all-concealing shadows. *"No!"* she said hoarsely, keeping her voice down as low as possible. "Don't shoot, L.J. He's working undercover. He's with us!"

A bullet exploded from the gun in a flash of lightning and was quickly followed by two more.

"NO!"

In stunned disbelief, she felt Ross's jerk of pain as the bullet hit him, heard the soft hiss that whistled through his tightly clenched teeth. She reached for him, her face ashen. "Oh, God, no! Ross!"

But before she could touch him, his arm swept around her waist like a steel band and dragged her back into the shadows of the shed as more shots rang out. "Keep down!" he ordered through gritted teeth. His shoulder burned as if someone had stabbed him with a white-hot branding iron. Cursing roundly, he reached for the reins of the mare, who had shied away in fright.

Suddenly all hell broke loose. The horses pushed at the gate of the corral in fright, threatening to break it down, and from the house came shouts of alarm. Over it all was the deadly echo of gunfire.

With a muffled oath, Ross practically threw Sam up in the saddle. Pain streaked through his right shoulder like a jagged edge of lightning. He ignored it and mounted behind Samantha, his arms encircling her as he gathered the reins in his right hand.

"Ross, your shoulder!"

"To hell with my shoulder," he gritted out, "we're getting out of here!"

The mare danced restlessly as he edged her toward the gate of the corral. From outside the shed, the shouts were getting louder, closer. Ross pushed Sam down until she was practically lying across the horse's neck. "Looks like we're going to have to be target practice, after all," he told her as he leaned over her and rested against her back. "Whatever happens, don't lift your head! Okay?"

Samantha nodded numbly and curled her shaking fingers into the mare's dark mane. Panic gripped her. She could feel the sticky wetness of Ross's blood on her back.

Ross reached for the latch on the gate and braced himself as the terrified horses crowded closer. "Hang on!" he shouted, and set the frightened animals free. They thundered out of the shed in a wild stampede, kicking up a cloud of dust, their nostrils flared with fear. They ran away from the gunfire, straight toward the house. The aliens who had stumbled out into the yard to see what was happening scattered like frightened chickens.

Ross's heels dug into the mare's flanks, his hands on the reins loose, giving her her head. She bolted, and they raced out of the shed at a full gallop, out into the moonlight with the other horses. Angry shouts and bullets whipped past their crouched figures as they shot past a surprised Raúl and Manuel and raced toward the protective darkness of the pines.

Chapter Eight

The thunder of pounding hooves was loud in Samantha's ears as they hurtled through the night. She clung to the horse's neck with fingers that ached with tension, her eyes wide and desperate, her heart in her throat as the shadowy shapes of trees and boulders loomed before them, then were quickly left behind. The uproar their escape had caused faded in the distance and finally died altogether. The night closed around them, and there was only the sound of their headlong flight and labored breathing.

Ross was shot! Outrage, confusion, worry hammered at her, pushing at the numbness that had dropped over her like a shroud when she'd felt him reel from the bullet. How could L.J. have done such a thing? She'd told him Ross was working with them; he must have heard her. Yet he'd deliberately tried to kill him. Had he lost his mind?

Her heart twisted in her breast, fear pulling at her as she felt the stiffness with which Ross held himself and the stickiness on her back. He was still bleeding. "Ross, you've got to stop and let me look at your shoulder. You're losing a lot of blood."

He didn't even check their reckless pace. "It's just a flesh wound," he said tightly. "You can bandage it when we stop."

"But—"

"Save it, Samantha," he cut in sharply. "We can't afford to stop. They'll come after us just as soon as they can round up some of the horses."

He was right. Her protests died in her throat.

Moonlight danced in and out of their path, dodging in between the pines, casting dangerous, all-concealing shadows. Ross guided the mare over the rocky ground with a steady right hand, clamping his teeth on the throbbing pain in his shoulder. With a will of their own, his eyes rested on Samantha's face as she sat tense and silent before him. Her hair teased his cheeks before the wind pulled it over his shoulder so that it flew out behind them. Her face was as pale as the moonlight, grave; her eyes were clouded with the horror of the nightmare that still chased them.

Something twisted inside him. The need to protect her, to wipe that look off her face almost became more than he could stand. He forced his fingers to hold the reins loosely. He couldn't stop and drag her against him; he couldn't take the time to kiss her until she forgot everything but him. Raúl and Manuel were probably already on their trail.

His eyes were hard as he turned his attention back to their surroundings. Moonlight turned the mountains ghostly white, softening their rugged terrain. But Ross knew them well. Even with the moon to guide him, these mountains were dark, dangerous, deadly. Soon the thickness of the pines would block out the moonlight and they would have to all but pick their way over the craggy ground. Speed would be nonexistent.

And the need for speed was all-consuming. His arms unconsciously tightened around Samantha. He wanted her out of Mexico. She'd been through enough. If he had any sense, he'd turn the mare around and head straight down the mountain to the desert and the river. It was the quickest route. It was also the most dangerous.

Determinedly he urged the horse higher up into the mountains.

The air turned colder, turning their breath to mist, and their reckless pace slowed. Ross's left arm grew heavy; without quite realizing it, he leaned against Samantha, fighting the pain that tried to dull his mind. When one of the mare's back hooves slipped on the smooth rock underfoot, he jerked to alertness, just barely saving the animal from stumbling. But fire streaked out from his shoulder in sickening waves. He groaned.

Samantha twisted around in alarm. ''Ross, your shoulder! Will you quit trying to act so tough! Stop and let me bandage it.''

"Can't," he replied through clenched teeth. "Don't have the time."

"Do you have the time to bleed to death?" She watched his jaw set stubbornly and wanted to shake him, but the pain clouding his eyes stopped her. Couldn't he see what he was doing to himself? She shifted sideways in the saddle and tried to reason with him. "Ross, you can't go on like this. If you think Raúl and Manuel are really coming after us, why are we going higher up into the mountains? Wouldn't it be faster to cut across the desert?"

He shook his head, clearing it. "Yeah, but Manuel will cover his bases. He'll send Raúl and some of the aliens up here while he waits in the desert. He's got a jeep down there he uses for trips back and forth to the river. The minute he spotted us, he'd shoot us down like rabbits."

A shiver raced up Samantha's spine. Now she knew what it was like to be hunted. Her eyes turned back to the vast emptiness of the mountains. If it wasn't for the fact that she knew they were being chased, she could almost believe they were the only two people in the world. "Won't they track us just as easily up here?" she asked softly.

"Not unless they get some dogs to sniff us out," he replied smuggly. "I know these mountains, Samantha, and for the past few miles, we've been traveling over rock. Don't worry, they won't find us."

But as the night slowly slipped away, it wasn't the smugglers that Samantha worried about. Ross leaned against her heavily, his head slipping down to rest on her shoulder. When his fingers grew slack on the reins, however, she grabbed at them in alarm and dragged the mare to a stop.

"I'm going to bandage that shoulder whether you want me to or not," she said fiercely, swiveling her shoulders around until she could see him clearly. The dark stain on his shirt was still wet. Her fingers reached for him, tears welling in her eyes. "Oh, you crazy man," she whispered huskily. "What are you trying to do to yourself?"

"Get you back across the river where you belong," he replied with a weak smile. He cupped her palm to his beard-roughened cheek. "Go ahead and do your worst, sweetheart. I'm too weak to fight you."

"You'll have to dismount—"

He was shaking his head before the words were even out of her mouth. "If I get off this horse, I may never get back on. You'll have to do it here."

She wanted to argue, but one look told her that only sheer determination was keeping him upright in the saddle. She pulled her shirttail out from where she had tucked it into her pants, then reached for the knife she had hidden in her pocket.

Ross lifted a brow at the sight of it. "Where'd you get that?"

"The kitchen," she replied with a quick grin as she cut a strip off her shirt. "Raúl was so busy laughing about my queasy stomach he never noticed when I slipped the knife in my pocket."

"And to think I was worried about you," Ross said with a laugh, shaking his head. "I should have known better."

"Yeah, you should have. I can take care of myself." She steeled herself to look at his blood-soaked shirt, furiously telling herself she was not going to get light-headed at the sight of his wound. She couldn't. He needed her.

And she loved him.

The thought came to her slowly, wrapping around her like a lover's arms, warming her, seducing her with an ache that was stronger than wanting, sweeter than need. How long? she mused with a soft smile. How long had she loved him? From that first breathless meeting of eyes?

She saw again the dark cove, the hard, unyielding glitter of his glare as his eyes had found her unerringly in the night. She'd lost her heart to him and had never even known it. Until now.

Sunshine bubbled in her like a brook. She loved him! How much that explained! She hadn't understood herself with him. She'd thought him a criminal, yet how effortlessly he had pulled passion from her. He made her forget right and wrong; in his arms she could forget the world. All she wanted now was the chance to care for him, to see to his comfort, his wounds, to chase the shadows from his eyes and urge forth the laughter that always caught her unawares. To love him.

But was that what he wanted?

The niggling thought intruded, unwanted. Ross de la Garza was a man who walked alone. She sensed it in the hard, unyielding set of his jaw, saw it in the secrets that clouded his eyes. He was a private man, a hard man who didn't like to let her see the softer side of him. Had he ever let himself need anyone?

With a flicker of unease, Samantha pushed the doubts away. He needed her now; she couldn't think about tomorrow.

With fingers that shook only slightly, she unbuttoned his shirt and gently pulled the material back to reveal his wound. The blood drained from her face. It was much worse, than she'd expected.

"I'll live, Red."

Her wide, distressed eyes lifted to his. She wasn't fooled in the least by his crooked smile. "You need a doctor."

"Probably," he admitted, surprising her. "But I'll make it without one. I have before. Bind me up, sweetheart, and let's go. We're wasting time."

"We could go across the desert—"

"No."

She wanted to argue. He'd lost so much blood that she didn't care about Raúl and Manuel anymore. She just wanted to get him to a hospital. But one look at his face had the words dying in her throat. He didn't have the strength to argue.

She cut another strip off her shirt and hurriedly folded it into a thick pad to press against the wound, worry etching her brow as she bound it in place. Stricken, she watched the blood immediately start to seep through. An awful feeling of helplessness curled into her stomach.

Do something! her heart cried. Don't just sit there and watch the life drain out of him!

Hurry. The word hammered in her head, prodding her, pushing her until the pounding of her heart echoed the ceaseless rhythm. She took the reins from Ross and urged his arms around her waist until he was once again leaning on her. "All right, we'll do it your way," she said softly, touching her heels to the mare to set the animal in motion again. "But if you die on me, Ross de la Garza, I'll never forgive you."

His chuckle was weak in her ear as he gave into the temptation to lay his head on her shoulder. "I'll try to remember that, Red."

The night was the longest of Samantha's life. Ross's low voice in her ear directed her westward, through mountain meadows that were sweet with the scent of the pure night air, over rocky cliffs that were terrifyingly silent in the darkness. Their progress was slow at best; when Ross's mind became dull with exhaustion and pain, it faltered altogether. Precious moments slipped away as Samantha tried to rouse him without letting him see the fear that nearly choked her. He was getting weaker.

"Ross, please, you've got to wake up," she pleaded desperately, pulling his slack arms around her waist reassuringly. "Do you hear me? Open your eyes and tell me which way to go. I think we're lost, and it's almost dawn."

Her voice came to him through the fog that obscured his brain. Ross frowned and struggled to reach her. "Sam?"

"Yes, yes! Oh, Ross, I was afraid—" She broke off suddenly and forced back her fears. He didn't need her fears. "Are you all right?" she finally asked with a calm she was far from feeling.

His frown deepened at the sound of strain in her voice, her need for him rousing him as nothing else could. "It's okay, love," he whispered roughly as he dragged his head up. "I'm still with you. Give me a chance to get my bearings."

They were on a narrow path that was little more than a track for the animals that roamed the mountains. Huge boulders crowded the path, and ragged peaks all but surrounded them, their rocky ledges catching the first golden rays of the sunrise that spilled over the horizon. It was cold, stark, beautiful. And in the eighteen years since he had last seen the region, it had somehow been left untouched by the hands of man.

Relief left him weak. With a tired smile, he leaned his head against Sam's. "No, we're not lost, sweetheart. We're home." Something akin to peace stole over him. No more running, no more shadows. How long had he been looking for that without even realizing it?

Confusion knit a line of worry between Samantha's brows. "Home?" she echoed. Was he hallucinating?

"See that big red rock over there to the left?" He pointed it out to her. At her nod, his arm dropped back around her waist. "Take the mare behind it. We'll be safe there."

Safe? Samantha wondered wildly. Was there such a place? A place where she could close her eyes and not know the horror of being tracked down like an animal? Not here, not now. She didn't know where she would ever feel safe again, and it certainly wouldn't be on this side of the Rio Grande.

But she couldn't tell him that, not when he was ready to drop. They rounded the rock, which was every bit as big as the smuggler's cabin had been, and stopped short. Samantha's hands automatically tightened on the reins. The opening of a cave yawned before them like the mouth of a whale.

"Ross?"

"Go ahead," he urged her. "You can ride the mare right inside."

Gingerly she did as he instructed, her eyes wide and wary as the dark, damp coolness swallowed them whole. She shivered, her pupils slowly adjusting to the shadowy interior. The cave wasn't as large or as dark as she'd first thought. As the sun edged its way higher up into the sky, the light from outside spilled inside, and she could see that the empty cave was only about twenty feet deep. A sigh slipped from her lips. No mountain lions here.

And he was right. For the first time in hours, she felt relatively safe. "How did you know about this place?" she asked as she pulled the horse to a stop. "From the outside, I didn't even know it was here."

"My father's ranch is right across the river," he told her quietly. "I grew up in these mountains." Gritting his teeth, he swung down from the saddle, and almost passed out as the move jarred his shoulder.

"Your father's ranch!" she echoed in surprise, landing beside him. "You never said...Ross! Oh, my God!"

He was waxen, the front of his shirt was covered in blood, and he clung to the saddle as if his legs couldn't support him. "Here, lean on me," she whispered hoarsely, and slipped her arm around his waist, taking care not to jostle his wounded shoulder. The fear and worry she'd been trying to hide all night exploded in angry words. "Why didn't you tell me you were bleeding this badly?" she cried as she took his weight and edged him toward the side of the cave. "I should have ignored you and stopped hours ago. To hell with Raúl and Manuel! Do you think I care about them when you're bleeding to death?"

Using all her strength, she helped him down to the cave floor, his back to the wall, his long legs stretched out in front of him. "Easy," she ordered in a voice laced with tears when pain rippled across the set lines of his face. "Damn it, Ross, you should have said something."

He leaned his head back against the rock wall. "I wanted to make the cave before sunrise." He couldn't seem to keep his eyes open. "Couldn't take a chance..."

"So you took a chance with your life, instead," she said flatly. With gentle fingers she pushed back a swath of dark hair that had fallen over his forehead. He was so pale. Her touch moved to his cheek, his arms. She couldn't stop touching him, reassuring herself that he hadn't slipped away. She couldn't lose him now, not when she'd spent her life looking for him.

Her hand came back to his cheek. "Don't go anywhere," she said huskily, forcing a smile. "I'll be right back. I'm just going to get the canteen."

She stumbled over to the horse on legs that were shaking with fear, and grabbed the canteen. But when she rushed back and fell to her knees at his side, his lashes were dark crescents against his bloodless cheeks. Samantha's heart stopped. *"Ross!"*

He struggled to lift heavy lids. "Right here, sweetheart," he murmured. "I'm still with you."

Her fingers fumbled with the cap of the canteen. "Here," she whispered, holding it to his mouth, "take a drink."

The cool water slid down his parched throat. He took it greedily, his hands closing over hers as he tilted the canteen higher. But when he finally dragged it away, he was weaker than before. "I'm as helpless as a baby."

"You'll feel better after I clean the wound and you get some rest," she assured him, silently praying she was right. "You're exhausted."

His fingers stopped hers before they even touched the rough bandage at his shoulder. He hated what he was going to have to tell her, but there was no other way. "You're going to have to take the bullet out, Sam."

Her eyes flew to his. "No!"

"Yes. You can do it."

No, she couldn't! She couldn't deliberately hurt him. Her fingers turned and gripped his. "I don't have anything to kill the pain," she argued stubbornly. "No soap to disinfect my hands. I'm afraid I'll hurt you more than you're already hurt."

"You're not afraid of anything." He squeezed her hand and flashed a teasing grin that was pathetically weak. "And as for hurting me, I know there's been more than one occasion when you wanted to kill me."

Her eyes welled with tears. "Oh, Ross."

"You can do it." He dropped her hand and reached for her, drawing her close for a kiss that was so soft, so tender, the tears in Samantha's eyes overflowed and slid down her cheeks. When he drew back he was smiling. "You can do it."

How could she argue with his confidence in her? She nodded. "All right."

Only sheer strength of will kept her fingers from shaking as she helped him lie down, then used some of the water from the canteen to wash her hands. She cut more of her shirt for bandages, uncaring that it now came only to her waist, and returned to his side. Her heart hammered against her ribs and fear was thick in her throat as she cut his shirt from his left shoulder.

Stricken, she looked at the rusty knife in her hand. "I can't use this."

Without comment, he reached into the pocket of his jeans and pulled out a pocketknife. Her fingers were shaking as she reached for it. "Tell me about this cave," she said desperately. "How did you find it?"

His eyes locked on her face. "My grandmother lived at the foot of these mountains. I spent as much time at her house as I did at my parents'." He felt her fingers dig at the wound with the knife and steeled his face to remain impassive. Sweat broke out on his brow.

She saw the muscle tick in his jaw and almost pulled back. She was hurting him! Horror washed over her as she blindly searched for the bullet. A sob rose in her throat. She couldn't find it! "Ross, I can't—"

"I ran wild up here," he cut in tightly. "I guess I was about nine when I discovered the cave. My father and I . . ."

He faltered, his voice dropping to a whisper. Samantha jumped as the knife blade suddenly brushed the slug. "Ross! Wait, I think I've found it!"

The pain that rolled over him threatened to drag him under like an undertow. He struggled to hang on to his train of thought. "Used it as a hunting base," he whispered.

"I've got it!" she cried, and pulled it out. Her shirt was damp with sweat, her fingers covered with blood.

They stared at the bullet in silence before their eyes automatically met over it. Ross tried to lift his hand to sweep the hair back from her face, but his arm suddenly weighed a ton. The pain pulled at him. He tried to smile. "Good girl," he said thickly, and quietly passed out.

"Ross!" With a quiet oath, Sam dropped the bullet and reached for him. His breathing was shallow under her hand. Relief almost left her giddy. She'd been terrified that the loss of blood and her clumsy fumbling had killed him.

The aftermath of the horror seeped into her until she was shaking in reaction. Get control of yourself, Samantha, she ordered herself sternly as she washed the wound again and bandaged it. There was no reason to fall apart now. It was all over.

She closed her eyes and took deep, cleansing breaths, but it was a few long moments before her legs were steady enough for her to stand. Exhaustion made her dizzy as she struggled to unsaddle the mare and give her a drink of water, but she forced herself to continue. Her eyes constantly drifted to Ross's still figure, and when she came to him and covered him with the horse blanket, he never moved. With a sigh, she stretched out next to him. She was asleep before her head touched the ground.

Interlude

Mac stared unseeingly at the paperwork littering his desk, his blunt features grim as he tried and failed to concentrate. With a muttered curse he reached for a cigarette. How was a man supposed to quit smoking when his guts were twisted with worry? Had they found her yet? Was she alive?

His head jerked up at the sound of a knock at his office door. "Come in," he barked.

David Martínez stepped inside, his eyes solemn as he closed the door behind him and turned to confront the older man. "Mac..."

"Where is she?" Mac demanded hoarsely. He shot to his feet and quickly came around the desk. "Is she okay? Did you have any trouble getting her away from those bastards?"

"She's not here," David admitted reluctantly. "I had to come back without her."

"What! Damn it, man—"

"She was escaping when we got there," David interrupted sharply. The usually soft lines of his broad face turned hard as the scene replayed in his head. "We were hiding in the dark, trying to decide what to do, when de la Garza pulled her into the shed where the horses were kept. He was helping her escape, but we didn't know that." His black eyes speared the older man's. "Damn it, Mac, you should have told us the man was working with us! Maybe things would have turned out differently."

Mac stiffened. "What happened?"

"We pulled our guns on him, and L.J. ordered him to release Sam," he explained grimly. "There was a full moon, and Sam must have seen our guns. She warned us he was on our side."

"And?" Mac prompted when he hesitated.

"L.J. shot him."

"He what?" Stunned disbelief turned the older man's face gray. He grabbed David's arms, his fingers fierce. "Are you sure?" he demanded hoarsely. "He shot Ross knowing he wasn't a smuggler?"

"Of course I'm sure," David snapped. "Do you think I'd make a mistake about something like that? He definitely hit de la Garza, but he was shooting at both of them. I couldn't believe it! It was as if he snapped. And when I asked him what the hell he was doing, he turned the gun on me!" He slumped into the nearest chair. "I had no choice, Mac," he continued quietly. "I had to kill him."

L.J. The informant. Mac leaned against the edge of his desk and tried to accept the news. He'd had his suspicions about L.J. when he escaped from the smugglers so easily and left Sam behind. But at one time or another he'd had suspicions about all of his agents. Now that he knew who the informant was, he found little satisfaction in the discovery. He was the one who sent L.J. back after Sam!

"Sam? And Ross?" he asked suddenly. "Where are they? Is Ross badly hurt?"

"They got away on one of the horses," David replied. "Once the shooting started, the smugglers came running out of the house, and I had to worry about saving my own neck. I took off and headed back across the river. I don't know where Sam and de la Garza are. I don't even know if they're alive."

Chapter Nine

Hours later, Samantha floated between consciousness and sleep, her body weightless with peace and warmed by the reassuring heat of Ross beside her. She lay on her side, holding him close, loving the feel of his long hard body pressed against her softness, drowsy contentment bringing a gentle smile to her lips. Her hand moved across his chest in a sleepy caress. There was an absolute rightness about being with him this way, lying next to him in the innocence of sleep. She could stay there the rest of the day and never want for anything but the feel of his arms around her.

Her hand moved over him dreamily, sliding over his ribs, the powerful strength of his chest, lingering at the buttons of his shirt, before unwittingly moving to his broad shoulders. Her fingers froze at the feel of the bulky bandage. She stiffened, and sleep vanished instantly. How could she have forgotten? she wondered as she bolted upright. She turned to him, unconsciously holding her breath, her eyes wide with the suddenly remembered horror of the night.

She searched his sleeping face, fear shaking her fingers as she reached for him. He was pale, and the dark hair that fell over his brow contrasted sharply with the ashen color of his skin. Her heart constricted in pain. He looked so tired, so sick; his breathing was shallow as his chest rose and fell in sleep. Did he have a fever?

Her touch was cool on his forehead, gentle as she brushed back his hair. Ross roused slowly, drifting from a sensual dream of her driving him mad with the touch of her hands and mouth to the reality of her bending over him. Caught up in the tantalizing heat of the dream, he smiled sleepily and pulled her down to him.

Their mouths met in a gentle meeting, lips softly parted, moist breaths mingling. It was a kiss of greeting, of morning, slow, languid, sweet, with just a taste of passion, a kiss where time stood still. Samantha forgot her worry, her fears for him, and let the pleasure seep into every pore, saturating her with enchantment, warming her until she felt her bones melt one by one. She could have kissed him like that for hours.

When she lifted her head her senses were swimming. "How do you feel?"

"Hungry for more," he growled. "Come back here."

She laughed shakily, her blue eyes sparkling as she resisted the urge to give into him. "Oh, no. You're in no shape for more than a kiss."

"Says who?" he countered, and pulled her hand to his mouth. The kiss he planted in her palm was tender, and surprised them both. He wasn't a man for romantic gestures. His eyes locked with hers. "I want to make love to you," he admitted quietly. "I have ever since I laid eyes on you."

His words brought an ache of longing to the very center of her being. It was what she wanted, too, what she'd fought from the very beginning. Even when she'd thought the worst of him she hadn't been able to stop herself from wanting him. Knowing that she loved him only made him that much harder to resist. Her fingers fluttered in his, then clung, her gaze meeting his unflinchingly. "No."

A dark brow lifted in surprise. "What do you mean no?" he demanded irritably. "You want me just as much as I want you. Don't pretend you don't. I was on the receiving end of that kiss."

He looked just like a little boy who'd been denied his favorite treat. Samantha bit back laughter just in time, but her eyes danced with it. "I'm not pretending anything," she defended herself. "But in case you've forgotten, you're not exactly in the best shape right now. You need your rest."

"I'm fine," he denied with a scowl, only to wince when pain clawed at his shoulder. His eyes closed weakly and his breath escaped in a ragged sigh. "It's just a flesh wound," he gritted out. "I'll be good as new in no time."

"Then we'll talk about this then," Samantha countered smoothly. "In the meantime, you need a doctor." She frowned at the dark shadows under his eyes, noticing them for the first time. "How far is the river from here?"

His eyes snapped open, entrapping hers. "A couple of miles. But don't get any ideas. We're not going anywhere yet."

He had to be the most stubborn man she'd ever met. "Damn it, Ross! You've not invincible. There's a very good chance the wound's already infected. You need a doctor."

"We're not moving until after dark," he retorted flatly. "A few more hours aren't going to make that much difference. Manuel and that partner of yours have probably been scouring the countryside ever since we got away. I'm not giving them a chance to find us."

Would L.J. really come after them? Of course he would. Had she ever really known the man? Feeling suddenly sick, she leaned her head back against the wall of the cave and clung tightly to Ross's hand. "Why, Ross? Why did he shoot you? Why did he try to shoot me? It makes no sense!"

Ross didn't have to ask who she was talking about. His fingers tightened reassuringly around hers. "He's the informant, sweetheart. Once he found out I was working undercover, he had no choice but to try to eliminate me. And you were a witness he couldn't afford. Thank God, he's a bad shot."

"Informant?" she echoed, confused. "Informant for who? I don't know anything about an informant."

"That's because Mac kept it under his hat. Someone at the station has been tipping off the smugglers for months. How else do you think they always seemed to just slip through your fingers? L.J. was obviously keeping them well-informed on the nightly stakeouts and roadblocks."

All the frustrations and anger of the past few months came rushing back—the mocking tracks, the long nights waiting for crossings that were taking place farther down the river. They'd tried everything they could think of to capture *Los Chisos*, but they'd always returned to the station empty-handed. How many times had she cursed her own incompetency? They all had. And all the time L.J. had been manipulating them like puppets.

"How could I have been so wrong about him?" she fumed. "I dated him, for God's sake! I should have been able to see through him."

"Why?" Ross challenged, scowling at the unfamiliar jealousy that knotted his stomach at the thought of her dating the man who had tried to kill him. "He fooled the whole station. You saw what you expected to see, what he wanted you to see—an agent who was just as frustrated and outraged by the smugglers as you were."

"That's why you were called in, wasn't it?" she asked shrewdly. "Mac couldn't trust any of us, so he brought in an outsider."

"I haven't been home in eighteen years, but I'm hardly an outsider," he said dryly. "I know this area like the back of my hand. And it wasn't that Mac couldn't trust you. He just didn't know who *not* to trust. Asking Washington for help wasn't easy for him.''

No, it wouldn't have been. For Mac that would have been admitting defeat. How he must have hated that! He wasn't a man who turned to others to solve his problems.

Her eyes drifted back to Ross, and found him watching her. "Who are you?" she demanded suddenly. "You're not an ordinary agent. Are you an agent at all? Why did Washington send you?"

"Because I'm damn good at handling difficult situations with a minimum of fuss. And Washington likes to keep these things quiet," he added mockingly. "They needed someone to slip in, crack the smuggling ring and then get out without causing an international incident. I've made a career out of doing that sort of thing."

He was a man who traveled the world looking for trouble. Her heart cringed at the thought, but she forced herself not to shy away from it. When the smuggling ring was cracked, when L.J. and the others were brought to justice, Ross would leave for Washington and then for parts unknown. She had to accept that.

She drew in a shuddering breath and ignored the emptiness that threatened to overwhelm her. "Did you discover who *El Chiso* is?"

"No." The answer was short, furious, gritted out through clenched teeth. The throbbing in his shoulder intensified to a burning ache. "I got everything but that."

Because of her. He didn't say it, but the words hung in the air between them nevertheless. His cover was blown and *El Chiso*'s identity was still a mystery. All he had to show for his hard work was a gaping hole in his shoulder.

"Ross, I'm sorry. I know that's lousy consolation, but—"

"If I could get my hands on that friend of yours for five lousy minutes, I'd drag the bastard's name out of him," he cut in fiercely. "That's the only good thing that's come out of this. As soon as we get back across the river and notify Mac, his cover will be shot to hell just as much as mine is."

"He's not my friend," she retorted in irritation. He obviously never had been. "And he's not stupid enough to let you get your hands on him. So what now?"

He sighed, suddenly exhausted. "We go to my old man's ranch and get in touch with Mac."

"You need to go to a hospital before you do anything," she said stubbornly.

He sighed in exasperation. "Sam, honey, you're not listening. My father's ranch is the only place we'll be safe. By now, L.J. has had time to tell *El Chiso* about us. He'll alert the entire smuggling ring, and they won't stop chasing us just because we cross the river. They'll try to stop us before we can get to Mac."

"You really think they'll stake out the hospital?" she asked in alarm. "And the station?"

"Don't you?"

Her blood chilled at the thought. Hadn't they already proved that their intentions were deadly? "Does

your father know that you've been working undercover?''

"No."

Samantha watched in surprise as the shudders
slammed down over his face, closing the subject,
closing her out. He gave a good imitation of a stone
wall. What had she said? She'd only asked about his
father.

I haven't been home in eighteen years, but I'm
hardly an outsider.

His words echoed in her ears. Eighteen years. Dear
God, he couldn't have been much more than a boy
when he left! Why had he never returned until now?
A dozen questions crowded her mind, but one look at
his face pushed them all aside.

He was pale with exhaustion and pain, and he was
running a fever. She should have noticed how quickly
he was tiring. Her palm cupped his cheek. The fear
that crept into her stomach was chilling. When his
hand moved up to hold her fingers against his face, she
struggled to find a smile for him. "Why don't you try
to sleep," she suggested softly. "You need to rest."

His eyes drifted closed despite his best efforts to
keep them open. "I don't seem to have much choice
in the matter," he complained weakly. "Wake me...at
dark.... And get you something...to...eat." He
fought to hang on to consciousness. He'd stashed
some food when he'd realized she was planning on escaping. He had to tell her. "Saddlebags..."

The fingers holding hers relaxed, but it was a long
quiet moment before Samantha left his side to check

his saddlebags. Tearful laughter spilled into her eyes at what she found there. Biscuits.

She stayed at his side all day, watching him, touching him, reassuring herself. The wall of the cave was cool against her back, the shadowy interior lit by the sunlight that heated the cave entrance as the sun dragged its way across the sky. She waited impatiently for the night.

But as time slowly slipped by, the absolute stillness of the mountains reached out to her, surrounding her, warming her, catching her unaware. How many times since she'd been assigned to the Presidio station had she sat in the dark and watched the river? In all those nights, she'd been too caught up in her job to let herself feel the timelessness of the land. She felt it now. It grabbed her, stealing her breath as she stared out the cave entrance at the hazy distant horizon to the north. Texas.

It was a vast land, a land of contrasts, of mountains and deserts, of violet shadows and sparkling sunshine. A land that time forgot. A smile pulled at her lips. It was said that if you looked hard enough in the Big Bend region of Texas, you could see the day after tomorrow. She could almost believe it.

No wonder Ross loved it. She'd heard the emotion in his voice when he'd spoken of this cave, of his grandmother and of hunting there with his father. These mountains were a part of him. Yet he hadn't been home in eighteen years. In all that time, had he forgotten the silence, the peace to be found here?

No, she decided. Once you'd seen this land, walked it, listened to it, it became a part of your soul. You might leave it, but you never lost the memory of how you felt there.

Hours later, long shadows fell across the cave entrance as the sun dropped behind the mountains, lowering the temperature ten degrees. Samantha shivered and rubbed her hands up and down her arms, desperately trying to hang on to the tranquillity that had helped her make it through the day. But she was fighting a losing battle and she knew it.

Ross was worse.

His skin was clammy under her fingertips, his skin color gray, his breathing shallow and ragged. He was restless, tossing about under the horse blanket, pain etching deep lines in his brow. A sick feeling of foreboding slid into Samantha's stomach. Was his wound infected?

Her fingers moved to his bandage to confirm her suspicions, but she hesitated, afraid to check it for fear the wound would start bleeding again. He'd lost so much blood already. He couldn't afford to lose any more.

The light finally failed altogether, and the fears she had been able to hold at bay during the light of day increased tenfold. The cave was pitch-black, cold, Ross's breathing labored. And outside, absolute silence reigned.

She wasn't a woman who scared easily—in her line of work, fear was a liability that could cost her her life. But when she turned to wake Ross and he lay unresponsive, she was terrified.

"Ross! Can you hear me? *Please*," she cried as she framed his face with her hands. "Wake up, sweetheart. You have to wake up!"

Ross groaned. A dull red haze of pain clawed at him with sharp talons, tugging him toward an oblivion that was dark, empty, painless. And never ending. It sucked at him, draining his will to fight.

Was she losing him? With a sob, Samantha ripped another strip off her shirt and quickly doused it with the water from the canteen. "It's Samantha, Ross," she pleaded, lovingly wiping his face with the wet cloth. "It's dark. It's time to go home."

Home. The word wavered in and out through the pain, teasing him. He frowned. The ranch...his father...Sam. Why was she crying? He lifted heavy lids and could just make out the shadowy outline of her bending over him in the dark. His eyes closed on a sigh. "It's dark."

"Yes," she breathed shakily, blinking back tears. "I...it is. The sun set about an hour ago." Her trembling fingers rested on his brow. "Ross, you're so hot. I think the wound's infected."

He found her hand in the dark. "I'm as strong as . . . a h-horse," he said faintly. His fingers tightened around hers. "Gotta go."

How would he make it to the ranch in this condition? she worried silently. He belonged in a hospital, not riding around the countryside. "Ross, can you ride? If you pass out, I won't be able to lift you."

"Help me up." He struggled to sit, cursing fiercely when a knife of pain twisted in his shoulder. "I can make it."

He somehow got into the saddle, but it was only through sheer strength of will and Samantha's support. They were both sweating freely when she mounted in front of him and took the reins. As she carefully walked the mare out of the cave, the cold night air rushed up to greet them.

Ross never noticed. Tongues of flame licked at him with each step they took, burning him from the inside out until he was only aware of the enervating, life-draining heat. It dulled his mind, drugging him. His arms tightened around Samantha's waist like steel bands.

"There's a path to the right of that big pine," he ground out between tightly clenched teeth. "Stay on it and it'll take you to the river."

She nodded, not trusting herself to speak, and did as he directed. The moon wasn't up yet, and it took all her concentration to stay on the steep rocky path. At her back she could feel Ross slipping in and out of consciousness. He groaned, and without quite realizing it, Samantha found herself talking, rambling, saying anything to keep him from slipping into the dark void of unconsciousness.

"Mac's going to be mad as hell when you show up with a hole in your shoulder. I can hear him now. 'Sheer carelessness.' And there's no telling what he'll have to say to me. Did you know he doesn't like women in the field? Never hesitates to let me know about it, either. We have an understanding. We both speak our minds without the other taking offense. Have you ever been married, Ross? I almost took the plunge once. Would have been the biggest mistake of my life."

She told him things she had never told another living being, hopes and dreams, disappointments, never waiting for an answer, desperately needing to give him a part of herself in the only way she could at the moment. When she told him she'd been swamped with loneliness and hadn't even realized it until she met him, his lips were soft against the side of her neck as he admitted he knew exactly what she was talking about. It had stunned him, too.

She'd never loved him more.

It took them hours to reach the river. By then Samantha's mouth was as dry as the desert from her nonstop talking, her arms knotted with tension from trying to keep the mare from jostling Ross any more than necessary. He seemed only vaguely aware of their surroundings as he leaned against her heavily, the heat from his body scorching her back.

Samantha stopped the mare at the river's edge, her eyes widening in distress. The water was muddy and swift, swirling and eddying, churning over hidden boulders as it raced madly toward the Gulf of Mexico. How could she possibly make the crossing with Ross in such bad condition?

Ross stirred, the impatient shifting of the mare jarring him into a consciousness blurred with pain. "What'sa matter?" he asked, slurring the words.

"The river's so swift here," she said with a worried frown. "Isn't there some place farther upstream that's calmer?"

"No. Quicksand," he murmured, killing her hopes. "Have to cross here."

Couldn't he see that it was too dangerous? "Damn it, Ross, you're not strong enough. If you were swept out of the saddle, you'd drown before I could reach you!"

"You're not getting rid of me that easily," he teased weakly. His arms tightened around her waist with a strength that surprised her. "Come on, Sam, you can do it."

What choice did she have? She dragged in a steadying breath, her fingers gripping the reins. "Just remember," she replied with a lightness she was far from feeling, "if you fall in, I'm pulling you out by your hair. I owe you that."

The water was cold, sucking at them, rising as high as their knees as the mare struggled toward the opposite bank. Although it wasn't that far, to Samantha it seemed a mile away. Her heart jumped into her throat, choking her. Ross's hold on her waist never slackened, but she was worried sick. They were both soaked now, shivering as the cool night air stroked them with icy fingers. How much more could he take before he collapsed?

When the mare finally struggled up on the opposite bank they were exhausted. Hot tears stung Samantha's eyes, and for one precious moment she held the horse still and let relief course through her. They had made it! Just a little farther and they would be safe, and Ross's father would see that Ross got the medical attention he needed.

"Which way now, Ross?"

The silence that answered her question chilled her to the bone. She stiffened, suddenly becoming aware of Ross's stillness, the harsh rasp of his breath, the stickiness of his blood on her back as his wound started bleeding again. He was unconscious.

Fear shot through her. This time she knew he wouldn't be weaving in and out of consciousness. Wildly her eyes scanned the darkness—and encountered only emptiness. Where was his father's house? A mile? Ten miles? Ross had said it was just across the river, but in this part of the country distances were measured in hundreds of miles. Ross could bleed to death before she found it.

She felt utter panic as her searching eyes swept the creosote-dotted terrain—and suddenly stopped. There, in the distance, was a light. Her heart thudded with hope.

Her eyes fixed on it unwaveringly as she urged the mare forward, never losing it in the darkness, not even when tears blurred her vision and ran down her cheeks. She wasn't even aware of it. Help was there, just out of her reach, pulling her toward the light. She headed straight for it.

It seemed to take an eternity to reach it. She was numb, oblivious to the cold night air and the stygian blackness that surrounded her, blind to the barns and windmills she passed as the light grew nearer, larger. Suddenly it was there before her, illuminating outbuildings, a garage, a house. A sob of relief shuddered through her.

A dog barked, sounding an alarm only seconds before it charged off the porch and ran toward the mare, growling furiously. The horse shied in fright, and it took all Samantha's strength to control it. She pulled back on the reins and gave the German shepherd a sharp order to go away, but the dog ignored her.

Ross's unconscious body suddenly started to slide off the mare. "Ross!" She grabbed at him, but he was too heavy, and the horse's nervous dancing only made the situation worse. Her fingers clutched at his arm ripping his shirt, catching only air. She watched in horror as he slid off the horse seemingly in slow motion and collapsed in a heap on the hard ground.

"Ross!" she screamed, and threw herself out of the saddle, pushing the mare away as she dropped to her knees in the dust next to his unconscious body. "Oh, God! Help! Somebody help me!"

Chapter Ten

Her cries brought the occupants of the house running. An elderly man quickly strode out onto the porch, his weathered face sharp and stern, his harsh command immediately silencing the dog. He was a lean, tall man, with gray eyes as sharp as an eagle's. As he looked at Samantha, her flaming hair wild and disheveled as she cried over a figure sprawled in the dirt, his surprise quickly turned to alarm. "What the hell!" he exclaimed, and started down the steps.

The screen door slammed. "What is it, Dad?" a younger man asked as he stepped outside. With hair as black as midnight and a perpetual sense of laughter molding the strong lines of his face, he was a softer, less mature version of Ross. Curiosity drew his dark brows together, and his handsome face was puzzled as his gaze followed that of his father's. "My God, somebody's hurt!"

The older man knelt in the dirt, not giving a thought to his neatly creased blue slacks as his big hands gently settled on Samantha's shaking shoulders and urged her back. "Here, miss, let me see—" He broke off, his eyes riveted on the blood that seeped through the bandage at Ross's shoulder. "Let's get him in the house, Adam," he barked. He glanced up to find the small, plump, white-haired woman who was his closest neighbor. Ginny always kept a cool head in a crisis. "Get the door, Ginny. We'll put him in the yellow guest room."

They all jumped to obey his orders, and before Samantha had time to more than brush the tears from her face, Ross was being carried inside.

Genevieve Nelson puffed up the stairs ahead of them, the pleated skirt of her lavender silk dress swishing with every step. She quickly pushed open a bedroom door. "Here, let me turn back the spread," she said softly as the two men carried in Ross's unconscious form. "Easy," she cautioned when they laid him on the bed. "He's awfully pale."

He was as white as the sheets. Samantha hurried into the bedroom after them, her blue eyes wide with distress, not even noticing the room's yellow-and-white decor as she stopped at the foot of the maple bed. "He's lost a lot of blood."

"Ginny, there are fresh bandages and antiseptic in the downstairs bathroom," the older man grimly said as he started to pull off Ross's dusty boots. "Would you get them? Adam, call Doc Taylor and tell him to get over here on the double.''

"Wait!"

Three pairs of shocked eyes turned to Samantha. "Please," she whispered, instinctively appealing to Ross's father in spite of his fierce frown. "The man who shot him is still chasing us. If he finds out where he is, he'll come after him. No one can know he's here."

The elderly man straightened to his full height of six foot two, his cool gray eyes narrowed dangerously. "Who are you?" he demanded suspiciously, pinning Samantha to the spot where she stood at the end of the bed. "And who are you running from?"

"My name is Samantha Spencer. I'm a border patrol agent." Her fingers twisted in agitation as her gaze shifted to the unconscious man on the bed. "Ross has been undercover with *Los Chisos*—"

The words died in her throat at the shocked gasps that followed her announcement. Puzzled, she watched in surprise as every muscle in Ross's father's body seemed to freeze.

John Larson's gaze swung back to the man on the bed in disbelief. Could this long-haired, bearded stranger be his son? He searched the pale features for some familiar sign of the young man who had left so many years ago, and felt his heart constrict in his chest. The curve of Ross's mouth, the high cheekbones... they were just like his mother's. "Ross," he whispered hoarsely, reaching for him. His fingers stopped just short of touching him.

It was that, more than the pain and regret she saw on the older man's face, that brought fresh tears to Samantha's eyes. He hadn't seen his son in eighteen years, yet something held him back from touching him. "Mr. de la Garza, I'm sorry," she said softly. "I thought you recognized him."

"No, I—" he broke off, a dark brow arching. "De la Garza? De la Garza was Ross's mother's maiden name. My name is John Larson."

Larson! Surprise left Samantha momentarily speechless. She should have realized that Ross was using an alias. He could hardly have posed as a smuggler using his real name, not when the Larson ranch was one of the largest in West Texas.

"Is it really Ross, Dad?" Adam Larson stood on the opposite side of the bed from his father, his brown eyes trained on the brother he could only vaguely remember. "I can't believe it! I'd never have recognized him."

John Larson shook off the shock that had gripped him ever since he'd recognized his eldest son and pinned his gaze on the youngest. "Yes. Now go call the doctor before he bleeds to death."

Ginny laid her hand on Samantha's arm reassuringly, her green eyes kind as she smiled at her. "It's all right, dear. Robert Taylor is an old family friend. In fact, he delivered Ross and Adam. You can trust him." At Samantha's hesitant nod, she patted her arm and followed Adam to the door. "I'll get the bandages now."

The silence in the room was thick with tension. When the older man turned back to Ross and started to undress him, Samantha moved to help. He shot her a sharp glance, but she met it unflinchingly and continued to work at the buttons of Ross's shirt.

"Who did this to my son?" he asked as he worked the wet jeans over Ross's hips and down his legs. "Do you know his name?"

Samantha dragged her eyes away from the man she loved, her cheeks tinged with color. She'd have had to be deaf not to recognize the fury in the old man's voice. "He'll be caught, Mr. Larson," she replied, deliberately sidestepping his question. "There's been enough shooting. Leave this to the authorities."

"The hell I will!" he snapped. "No one shoots a Larson and gets away with it. I want that name, Ms. Spencer."

"Samantha," she corrected as she pulled the knife from her pocket and split Ross's right sleeve from the cuff all the way to the collar. She tossed the shirt on top of his jeans and pulled the covers up to his waist before she straightened and calmly confronted Ross's impatient father.

"That's privileged information, Mr. Larson. Ross insisted we come here because he knew we'd be safe, not because he wanted you to take on his battles."

She watched impatience struggle with indignation in the gray eyes that were so like Ross's and waited for the explosion that was sure to come. Of course he didn't have any idea how much he and his son were alike. He hadn't seen him in eighteen years. He couldn't know that Ross had his same ability to take charge in a crisis, that giving orders came as naturally to him as breathing and that he, too, didn't take kindly to anyone questioning his authority. Thirty years from now, Ross would have that same distinguished gray at his temples, that same proud bearing that wouldn't stoop to age. She smiled fondly. Such stubborn men. She was going to like John Larson.

"You're not going to tell me, are you?"

"No."

His frown turned into a scowl. "What give you the right to speak for my son?"

"I love him," Samantha answered simply, admitting it aloud for the first time. "And I think I know him well enough to know that he wouldn't want his father risking his life for him."

He digested that in silence, his eyes solemn as they rested on Ross. When he lifted his head, the anger was gone. "How did you meet him?"

"He kidnapped me."

Surprise, then a laughter that was totally unexpected warmed his gray eyes. Samantha sensed he was not a man who smiled easily. "That figures," he said wryly. "He was a handful as a boy. I see he hasn't changed." He looked as if he wanted to say more, but then Ginny bustled into the room with Adam on her heels, and the moment was gone.

"Doc Taylor will be here in about fifteen minutes," Adam told his father. "I explained the situation to him, and he said he'd make sure he's not followed."

The older man nodded. "Good, but we've got to stop the bleeding before then." Ginny moved to his side, laying scissors and gauze on the side of the bed as John carefully removed the bandage. At the sight of the wound he stiffened. "When did this happen?" he asked roughly.

"Last night," Samantha answered quietly. Her insides knotted with fear. Ross hadn't moved since they'd laid him on the bed. "It took all night to get away from the smugglers, and Ross refused to risk crossing the river during the day. I kept telling him he needed a doctor, but he wouldn't listen to me."

"Stubborn fool," his father murmured angrily.

"He did what he had to do, John," Ginny said quietly, touching his arm reassuringly. "He's your son. You wouldn't have expected any less of him."

"We crossed as soon as it was dark," Sam continued. "He's been unconscious since then."

John pressed a clean bandage to the wound after cleaning it with the antiseptic Ginny provided, his eyes never leaving his son's face. "He's going to be all right," he said fiercely. "Robert will stitch this up in no time and fill him with antibiotics. He'll be fine."

Samantha wasn't sure who he was trying to convince, but there were doubts written on all their faces. She watched him secure the new bandage and found herself wringing her hands. She felt so helpless!

"Would you like to clean up, Samantha?" Ginny asked as she picked up the remains of the supplies she had brought upstairs. "We were just finishing dinner. If you'd like something to eat while we're waiting... You must be hungry."

"No... I don't want to leave Ross, Mrs.—"

"Ginny, dear. Ginny Nelson. I'm a neighbor." She handed the supplies to Adam before taking Samantha's arm and leading her to an overstuffed chair.

"Why don't you sit?" she suggested. "I know you're worried sick about Ross. We all are. But you can't neglect your own health. You'd be surprised how much brighter the future will look after a bath and something hot to eat."

Samantha automatically settled in the chair, and for the first time since Ross had been carried into the house, she noted that Ginny's dress was silk and the Larson men were obviously dressed for a small dinner party. Chagrined, she looked down at her own clothes.

Her slacks were wet and filthy, encrusted with dirt from the knees down. What remained of the shirt Ross had loaned her was splotched with blood and just barely covered her breasts. Heat suffused her cheeks. "Oh, Lord, I'm a mess. I hadn't realized..."

Ginny chuckled, her green eyes twinkling with understanding. "After what you've been through, I'd say you're entitled. When Ross is better, I'm looking forward to hearing all about it."

"Me, too," Adam said enthusiastically, his grin less cynical than Ross's but achingly familiar. "It must have been exciting."

"It was terrifying," Samantha replied solemnly. Her eyes lingered on Ross. "I was so afraid he was going to die before I could get him to a doctor."

"Robert will be here any minute," John Larson assured her. "You don't have to handle this alone any longer, Samantha."

How had he known how lost she felt? How inept? Tears gathered in her eyes. "Thank you," she whispered thickly.

The sudden barking of the dog was like the ringing of an alarm. "That's Doc Taylor," Adam announced, and hurried downstairs, the gauze and scissors forgotten in his hands.

He was back within seconds, followed by a short, white-haired man dressed in a natty three-piece gray suit, his wire-rimmed glasses sliding down his nose, a black medical bag in his hand. He immediately went to the bed and lifted Ross's wrist, his fingers on the pulse. "Fill me in, John."

Ross's father turned to Samantha. "I think Samantha can do that better than I," he told him. "She's been with Ross since he was shot."

She began haltingly, telling him of the long flight in the mountains, Ross's insistence that she remove the bullet, the blood he had lost. And all the time she talked, Robert Taylor's hands moved over Ross skillfully, gently, knowingly. Samantha let the tension slowly drain from her with a sigh. This was a man who knew what he was doing and who cared.

A frown drew the doctor's white brows together as he listened to Ross's heart with a stethoscope. He pulled the instrument from his ears and turned to confront the anxious eyes that watched him. "Will you all please wait downstairs?" he said in a firm voice. "John, I'll need your assistance."

"I'd like to stay," Samantha said quietly. Her eyes met those of the doctor. "Please."

He picked up her wrist without comment, his blue eyes watching her carefully, missing little as he scanned her ashen cheeks and violet shadowed eyes. He shook his head, his smile kind but leaving little room for ar-

gument. "You've had a rough few days, young lady.
I'll do everything I can for Ross, and you can do the
same. Falling apart won't help him. Go get some rest.
He's in good hands."

He was right, of course. But that didn't make the
leaving any easier. She went reluctantly, her eyes
clinging to Ross until the last minute. At the door she
told the doctor, "Call me, please, when you're finished. I want to sit with him." At his nod she followed Ginny into the hall.

"How about something to eat now?" the older
woman asked with a smile. "It'll occupy the time, if
nothing else, while we wait."

"Actually," Sam admitted, "I'd love a bath. But I
don't have any clean clothes." She wrinkled her nose
in distaste as she plucked at her shirt. "I couldn't stand
to put these back on."

A beautiful smile spread across Ginny's finely lined
face, understanding brightening her eyes. "You leave
that to me. I might not be able to find you anything
but one of Adam's shirts, but I'll guarantee you it will
cover you more than that one does."

"I hope so," Samantha said with a laugh. "I hadn't
realized just how indecent this one had become. But I
had to use it for bandages..."

The older woman watched her smile fade and hurriedly pushed open a door farther down the hall. "You
can bathe in here," she said, revealing a blue-tiled
bathroom. "And I'll go find you something to wear."

What she found was an old red football jersey of
Adam's that clashed horribly with Samantha's hair
and fell below her knees, swallowing her whole. Sa-

mantha couldn't help but laugh when she saw herself in the mirror. "Well, it's certainly big enough," she said dryly. "I could get lost in this."

With a grin Ginny handed her a robe. "Tomorrow I'll run into town for you, if you like, and pick up a few things. But this will have to do for tonight. It's the smallest thing I could find. Adam wore it in *junior* high school. The Larson men aren't little."

"So I'm finding out." Sam giggled as the robe pooled at her feet. "As long as I don't trip on the hem, I'll be fine."

"Good. Then let's go downstairs. Adam is fixing you an omelet and it should be just about ready."

Samantha was convinced she wouldn't be able to eat a bite. How could she, when Ross lay unconscious upstairs? But when Ginny pushed open the swinging door that led to the kitchen, and the heavenly scent of the omelet teased her senses, she was suddenly ravenous. She hurriedly took a seat at the glass-topped kitchen table and reached for a fork the minute Adam set the food in front of her.

"Nice outfit," he teased as he took the seat across from her. When she only flashed him a quick grin and continued eating, his lips twitched traitorously. "Did you have *anything* to eat today?"

"Biscuits," she admitted ruefully, forcing herself to slow down. "Ross had stashed them in the saddle-bags." She took a sip of the coffee Adam had brewed, sighing in appreciation. "This is wonderful. I hadn't realized how hungry I was. I've been so worried about Ross—"

"He'll make it, Samantha," he said confidently, frowning at the shadows that suddenly clouded her eyes. "I know you've been through hell, but it's over."

If only it were that easy, she thought wistfully. She laid her fork back on the plate, her appetite deserting her. "It won't be over until *El Chiso* is captured," she corrected him quietly. "Ross won't be safe as long as that man is still loose."

"Does he know who it is?" Ginny asked as she refilled Samantha's cup with coffee. "Maybe it's just a matter of time..."

Samantha shook her head. "No. He was getting close, but then I was captured, and he had to blow his cover." She toyed with her coffee before finally pushing it away. Sighing heavily, she came to her feet. "I've got to call Mac at the station and let him know what's happened. Is there a phone I can use?"

"The one in the study," Adam answered promptly. "It's right off the living room."

She found the study easily. It was a small room, private, with book-lined walls and a beautiful walnut desk that immediately drew the eye. It was cluttered with ledgers and correspondence, and Samantha could easily picture John Larson sitting there in the evenings, catching up on paperwork. Taking a steadying breath, Samantha sank into the tufted leather chair behind the desk and reached for the phone.

Mac picked it up on the second ring. At his sharp hello, Samantha blinked back a sudden rush of foolish tears. The old codger. She wished he were there so she could hug him. "Hello, Mac," she said softly. "This is Samantha."

"*Samantha!* Where are you? Are you all right? Damn it, girl, answer me!"

He practically shouted the rapid-fire questions at her, until Samantha had to hold the receiver away from her ear in self-defense, a slow smile stretching across her face. "I'm fine, Mac. I'm at the Larson ranch."

"Larson ranch," he echoed, his voice suddenly grim. "Ross? How is he? I know he was shot when you were trying to escape."

"He's . . . not good. He's unconscious. A doctor's with him now." Her fingers tightened on the phone. "Mac . . . L.J. shot him. And he knew Ross was working with us!"

"I know." His sigh was heavy and filled with self-disgust. "I'm the one who should've been shot—for sending him after you. He could have killed you both and I'd have been none the wiser if David hadn't been with him."

"David! David was with him?"

"Yes," he growled, "and it's a good thing, too. He was stunned when L.J. shot Ross and then tried to shoot you. He had no choice but to kill him."

L.J. was dead. Samantha reeled at the news, the words echoing in her head. She should have felt satisfaction that justice had been done, that he was no longer a threat to either her or Ross. Instead all she felt was an overwhelming sadness. "I'm sorry," she said quietly.

"After he tried to kill you!" Mac thundered, outraged. "Don't you dare feel sorry for him. He betrayed you and everyone else, and if *El Chiso* finds out

Ross is at the ranch, his life won't be worth a plug nickel. And neither will yours.''

"He's not going to find out," she stated firmly. "The doctor is a family friend, and no one else knows we're here but the family and a neighbor, Ginny Nelson.''

"Ross has mentioned her. She's been friends with John Larson for years. But you're not going to be able to leave the ranch until it's safe. You got that?''

"But Mac, I'm not a threat to *El Chiso*! The only smugglers I could identify are Raúl and Manuel.''

"You've been to their hideout, Sam," he pointed out. "And at this point, *El Chiso* doesn't know what Ross may have told you. What *did* he tell you?''

"Nothing. Only that he was very close to learning who *El Chiso* is.''

"Damn," Mac growled softly. "I was counting on Ross to nail that bastard.''

"He would have, Mac, if it hadn't have been for me," Sam replied. "I really screwed things up.''

He scowled at her depressing tone. "Don't start crying on me, Spencer," he said gruffly. "You were only doing your job. Ross hasn't been spinning his wheels the past few months. He may not have discovered *El Chiso*'s identity, but you can bet your paycheck, he's sweating it out now, wondering just what he did find out. You call me just as soon as Ross is able to talk to me. And don't you dare leave that ranch!''

Nothing on earth would make her leave Ross. "Don't worry, Mac, I'm not going anywhere.''

Ginny stuck her head around the door just as Samantha was hanging up. "Oh, good, you're finished," she said with a smile. "Dr. Taylor would like you to come into the living room, dear. He'd like to talk to all of us about Ross's condition."

Samantha's nerves knotted in her stomach, but she got hurriedly to her feet, tightening the belt of her robe before following the older woman into the living room.

It was a long, comfortable room, with a colonial-style red plaid couch and matching chairs flanking a huge rock fireplace. A gold braided rug and drapes at the wide window that looked out over the front yard made it cozy and warm. Samantha perched on the edge of the couch, unknowingly looking like a nervous child in the huge robe and football jersey, her hair flowing down her back to her hips.

John Larson settled into his favorite easy chair as Ginny sat next to Sam. Once Adam had taken the other chair, he looked at the doctor inquiringly. "Well, Robert, how is he?"

"He's lucky to be alive," he replied bluntly, his round face grim. He pulled a handkerchief from his pocket and carefully polished his glasses before he looked up. "He needs to be in the hospital." When Samantha opened her mouth to protest, he held up his hand, cutting her off. "I realize that's not possible. I just want you to realize the seriousness of Ross's condition. It's critical."

The blood drained from Samantha's cheeks, bringing the doctor a momentary pang of regret for his bluntness. "He has you to thank for being alive, my dear," he said gently. "The bullet came damn close to his heart. He'd be a sorry sight now if you hadn't been there to help him. As it is, he's got a serious infection."

"So what's your prognosis, Robert?" John Larson asked quietly.

The doctor returned his handkerchief to his pocket and spread his hands helplessly. "I've done everything I can for him, John, short of taking him to the hospital. The next thirty-six hours are critical. The wound's infected, and he's running a high fever. He'll have to be watched carefully." He reached for his black medical bag. "I'll be back in the morning to change the bandage and give him some more antibiotics. If there's the slightest change in his condition before then, call me immediately."

The atmosphere in the living room was solemn as John stepped out onto the porch to escort the doctor to his car. Adam came to his feet and paced restlessly, his hands shoved into his pocket. "I'll stay with him tonight," he volunteered. "We'll have to arrange shifts—"

Samantha came swiftly to her feet, her jaw set determinedly. "I'd like to take the first shift."

"Come on, Samantha, be reasonable," he argued, frowning. "Look at you. You're dead on your feet. You're in no shape to stay up all night."

"I wouldn't sleep, anyway, Adam. I'd be too worried to even close my eyes."

"I don't think it would hurt for Samantha to sit with Ross for an hour or two," John Larson said quietly from the doorway. "Do you, Adam?"

"But, Dad—" he protested, only to stop at the stern light in his father's eye. "I was only thinking of Samantha," he defended himself stiffly. "She's exhausted."

"She'll sleep much better after seeing Ross," his father assured him. "Then you can take over for the rest of the night. Is that all right with you, Samantha?"

"Yes." She let out a sigh. "Thank you. I just need to make sure he's okay."

Ginny rose gracefully to her feet and gave her a brief, encouraging hug. "We understand, dear. Go on up."

That was all the encouragement she needed. She hurried up the stairs and let herself into the yellow guest room, silently shutting the door behind her. For one long endless moment, she just stood there, her heart in her eyes as she stared at him.

He was still incredibly pale, his lashes dark smudges against his unnaturally white cheeks as he lay on his back, the covers drawn up to his chest. The bandage at his shoulder was a new one, professionally applied and infinitely reassuring.

The nerves that had kept her going for so long were suddenly shaky, and tears threatened to mist her eyes. She stiffened, ruthlessly forcing them back. The battle he fought now had nothing to do with the smugglers, and he needed her strength, not her tears.

She made herself move away from the door and crossed the room to carefully sit on the side of the bed. Unconsciously her fingers moved to touch, to soothe. And although she knew he probably couldn't hear her, she began to talk to him as she had on the horse, opening her heart to him.

"I love you," she whispered huskily. "By whatever name you go by. Ross de la Garza. Ross Larson. It doesn't matter. I've spent an eternity looking for you and didn't even know it. I can't let you slip away from me now that I've found you. Do you hear me, Ross?" Her palm cupped his cheek, urging him to hear, to fight. "I love you, and you're not going to die. I won't let you!"

Chapter Eleven

Time moved grudgingly. Minutes at last turned into hours, the sun rose in the cloudless West Texas sky, yet to Samantha it seemed like an eternity since she had arrived at the ranch. It had been a long night and was an even longer day. Ross wandered in and out of consciousness, with his condition remaining virtually unchanged. Every eight hours they changed shifts, and although they told one another that Ross's color was better, they really didn't believe it. By the time evening arrived, the tension in the house was like a powder keg waiting to explode.

Samantha had stayed at Ross's side even when it wasn't her shift, taking breaks only when it was absolutely necessary, but the strain was the most telling on John. Worry had furrowed deep lines in his forehead, and his mouth was tight and grim. He seemed as if he had aged a decade overnight, and suddenly he looked every one of his sixty-nine years. Ginny watched him with troubled eyes.

"John Larson, you have to take better care of yourself," she scolded, her hands resting on her jean-clad hips as she stood at the kitchen counter, fixing a tray for Adam, who was taking his turn sitting with Ross. Her softly rouged lips tightened with disapproval when John only picked at his dinner. "You're worrying yourself to death!"

He frowned down at the roast and potatoes she had cooked and pushed it away. "Don't nag, Ginny. I'm not worrying. I'm just not hungry."

"Bull!"

Samantha bit back a smile. Ginny was a godsend. With gentle badgering, prodding and her ever-ready smile, she had fussed over them all like a mother hen. Whenever any of them needed something—food, words of encouragement, a hug—she was there. She'd even gone into town and bought Samantha the jeans and yellow cotton blouse she now had on so that she'd have something to wear until it was safe for her to return to her apartment.

"I beg your pardon?" John asked, a dark brow lifting inquiringly.

"You heard me," Ginny replied pertly. "Bull! Who do you think you're fooling? You spent half the night pacing the floor, and this morning you hardly touched your breakfast. If you keep this up, we'll have another patient to take care of."

"Don't be ridiculous," he growled irritably. "You're exaggerating."

Samantha silently disagreed with him. Ginny wasn't exaggerating. She was concerned, and she had a right to be. She loved him. It was there shining in her eyes, in her smile, and especially in her frown. Samantha could only marvel that John Larson didn't see it. Ginny had promised to stay and help until Ross was out of danger, but Samantha knew the older woman wanted to be there to comfort John and protect him from the strain as much as possible.

John wasn't making it easy. When he ignored her grumblings and came to his feet, she glared at him in exasperation. "Where are you going?" she demanded suspiciously.

"Upstairs. I'll take Adam's tray up to him—"

"No, *I'll* take it up," she interrupted sternly. She lifted the heavy tray without blinking an eye and carried it to the door, which she pushed open with her hip. Her snapping green eyes dared John Larson to so much as take a step out of the kitchen. "You sit down and rest, damn it!"

"Yes, ma'am," he replied meekly, winking at Samantha.

"Humph!" the older woman snorted, not fooled in the least. With one last blistering look, she let the door swing shut behind her.

Samantha's brows shot up at the sound of John Larson's chuckle. A rare grin spread across his face. "Ginny can be tough as nails when she wants to be."

When he smiled like that, Samantha could see why Ginny loved him. "She's right, you know," she told him quietly. "You should let Adam and me shoulder more of the responsibility. You're wearing yourself out."

"And what about you?" he countered swiftly. "We've had to practically pull you away from Ross's side."

"I'm holding up fine," she replied, shrugging off his concerns.

He cursed softly, the stern lines of his weathered face looking remarkably like his eldest son's as he scowled at her. "You're as stubborn as Ross."

Samantha's lips twitched. "Perhaps. Ross can be the Rock of Gibraltar when the mood strikes him. Who do you think he gets that from?"

His expression didn't change by so much as a flicker of an eyelash, but Samantha was almost sure she detected a twinkle of laughter in the cool depths of his gray eyes. "Are you implying that I'm stubborn?" he asked silkily.

"Yes."

A slow grin worked its way across his face. "You may be right. I guess Ross comes by it honestly."

Like father, like son. The old maxim had certainly proved true. John took a quick sip of coffee, his eyes reflective, trained on the past. Ross had been his shadow, dodging his footsteps every chance he got, walking like him, talking like him. Then suddenly they'd done nothing but argue and fight.

The laughter softening the older man's chiseled face suddenly flickered and died. "Maybe that's why the two of us always seemed to be at each other's throats," he said half to himself. "Especially after Olivia died."

"His mother?" Samantha asked softly.

"Yes." He sighed heavily. "It was a difficult time for all of us, but especially for Ross. He and his mother were very close, and he lost her at a time when he really needed her softness. And I couldn't see that."

The agony that tore at him twisted Samantha's heart. So much pain had built up over the years. "You were grieving, too, John."

"I was numb," he admitted in a voice thick with pain. "Lost. And Ross suddenly didn't give a damn about anything. He started running wild, taking stupid chances. We argued all the time." He clenched his jaw in an obvious attempt to regain control of his emotions. When he finally spoke, his voice was expressionless. "I was worried about what he was doing to himself, how he was influencing Adam. I finally had enough, and one night we had it out. I laid down the law and told him in no uncertain terms exactly what I expected of him. He was going to go to college, graduate, then help me run the ranch."

Samantha winced. Even at eighteen, Ross would not have taken an ultimatum lightly. "What happened?"

"He told me he was joining the army and shaking the dust of West Texas off his feet for good. I was livid. I told him not to bother ever coming back if he was going to abandon his responsibilities here."

"So he didn't come home for eighteen years."

He shot her a surprised look. "He told you?"

"He didn't give me any details, just that he'd left eighteen years ago." How much he had left unsaid. "Ross is a very private man. He doesn't talk about the past."

"It was my fault," his father said bluntly, his face grim. "I had no right to try to take charge of his life that way. He was eighteen, a man, and he reacted as any man would when given an ultimatum."

His chair screeched in protest when he pushed it back abruptly and came to his feet, turning to the kitchen's wide-paned windows. Blindly he stared out over the arid, seemingly endless acres of his ranch, his clenched fists shoved into the pockets of his khaki pants. "Ross had a lot of pride, even at that age," he continued hollowly. "I had no one to blame but myself when he took me at my word and didn't come back. I didn't make the same mistake with Adam. Now I don't know if I'll ever get the chance to tell Ross just how wrong I was."

"Don't say that!" Samantha protested fiercely. She jumped to her feet and came swiftly to his side, her fingers curling into his arms as she resisted the urge to shake him. "He needs you now more than ever. He's always needed you, even when he was too stubborn to admit it. Don't you dare give up on him. He's going to make it."

She believed that with all her heart—she wouldn't allow herself to believe anything else. But during the long, lonely hours after midnight, doubts crept in, and it became increasingly difficult to hang on to her optimism. Dr. Taylor had arrived after dinner, and although he was encouraged because Ross's vital signs were stable, the persistent fever that he hadn't been able to shake had the older man worried. The antibiotics weren't working as well as he'd hoped.

The house was silent as a tomb; everyone had long since gone to sleep. Downstairs a clock softly chimed two. From her position in the overstuffed chair near the bed, Samantha tried to concentrate on the murder mystery Ginny had guaranteed her was a page turner, but her eyes kept wandering to Ross.

The light from the reading lamp on the nightstand bathed the room in a soft glow. Ross moved restlessly under the sheet that covered him, and Samantha's eyes snapped to him in alarm. She held her breath, her heart knocking against her ribs as she waited for him to slip back into sleep. He mumbled hoarsely and tossed his head back and forth on the pillow.

She jumped up with a startled cry, the book falling unheeded to the floor as she ran to his side. "Ross!" Her hand went to his brow. "My God, he's burning up!"

His cheeks were crimson with fever, and heat radiated from him. He kicked at the sheet, his low moan loud in the room's deathly quiet as he knocked her hand away.

The blood drained from Samantha's cheeks. Stricken, she tried to think. He was so hot! Dr. Taylor had warned them they would have to cool his body down if his temperature became any higher. If wet towels didn't work, he'd have to be carried to the bathtub.

She found a small stack of towels on the dresser, along with a bowl of cool water. Hurriedly she reached for them, a sob tearing at her throat as she jerked the covers away and hastily sat the bowl on the nightstand before saturating the towel in the water. She never noticed the water that sloshed onto the floor as she quickly squeezed out the cloth and carried it to his hot face.

"No, don't!" she cried when he turned his head away with a harsh murmur. "You must lie still, Ross. Let me cool you off."

If he heard her, he gave no sign. His dark head tossed fitfully on the pillow, and his feverish mumblings were unintelligible. Panic shook Samantha's fingers as she frantically returned the towel to the water and then moved it down the strong column of his neck, over his broad shoulders and across his chest.

Over and over she repeated the procedure, losing count of the times she doused the cloth, never noticing the ache in her back as she hovered over him, blind to the growing tiredness of her hands. She stroked his back, his face, his arms and legs, praying aloud and not even knowing it.

Downstairs the clock chimed three.

She moved to wipe his bearded face again, and suddenly found her wrist manacled by his fingers. Her startled eyes flew to his and found him staring at her with the cold angry eyes of a stranger. "How did you get in here?"

Samantha paled at his furious demand. "Ross?"

"Don't try that innocent act on me," he sneered. "Who sent you here?"

"Ross, it's me, Samantha," she pleaded, unable to hold back a cry of pain when his fingers tightened threateningly around her wrist. "You're at your father's ranch. Don't you remember?"

"It doesn't matter, anyway," he continued as if she hadn't spoken, tossing her hand away distastefully. "I haven't got the documents, sweetheart, so you're wasting your time. Someone got there before I did. Probably one of the rebels." The hostility that sharpened his features suddenly vanished, and with a groan he turned away from her, his eyes closing wearily. "Damn, it's hot."

He was hallucinating! A fear unlike any Samantha had ever known curled into her stomach. "Ross, you've been shot," she explained desperately. "You have an infection and I'm trying to bring your fever down. Do you understand?"

His only answer was a disjointed mumbling.

Again she wet the towel in the cool water, unconsciously steeling herself for another violent reaction when she brought it to his hot skin. But he never moved. Her breath slipped out on a sigh of relief.

She wasn't sure when the fever first changed to chills. One minute she was moving the washcloth over him, deliberately numbing her brain so she wouldn't panic, and the next he was shaking.

For a moment she was too stunned to do anything but stare at him in dismay. There were goose bumps on his skin, and his teeth were clenched against a cold that came from within. Shivers violently shook his powerful frame. Samantha dropped the cloth back into the water and frantically reached for the comforter lying at the foot of the bed.

She packed the covers around him, but the shaking continued, and she knew with a sick feeling of fear that this wasn't something she could handle alone. She had to get someone to call Dr. Taylor.

"Sam?"

The hoarse whisper stopped her as she was halfway to the door. She whirled. He watched her with eyes bright with pain, but alert and lucid. "Ross, I've been so worried about you! I was just going to call the doctor—"

"Don't leave me." The plea was faint, taxing, seeming to take everything out of him. His eyes drifted closed.

"But, Ross..." She hesitated, her teeth worrying her lower lip. She knew the doctor should be updated on his condition, but she also knew that she couldn't leave him, not when he had just asked her to stay.

She reached over to tuck the comforter more closely around him, only to stop when another shiver racked his helpless body. She had to get him warm. Then she could alert the family, and they could call the doctor. Her hands went to the belt of the robe Ginny had found for her the previous night.

When she slid into bed beside him she doubted if he was even conscious of her huddling against him, her arms wrapped around him, the red football jersey riding up to her hips as her bare legs entwined with his. She held him close, willing her body heat to soak through his skin and warm him, her insides twisting every time a shudder ran down his lean frame.

They lay like that for what seemed like an eternity, the covers pulled up over their shoulders, the sound of their breathing whispers in the silence. The clock chimed another hour, but Samantha heard only the steady reassuring beat of Ross's heart against hers. Her arms grew tired, then ached from the tightness of her hold on him, but she wouldn't allow herself to weaken, not even for a second. She prayed as she had never prayed before.

His chills left him as abruptly as they had begun. Suddenly he was still, and Samantha's heart stopped in alarm. She pushed herself up until she was leaning over him, her blue eyes wide as she searched his face. He was asleep, his breathing slow and steady, beads of sweat dotting his brow. Her trembling fingers touched his forehead. It was cool.

"The fever's broken." She whispered the words in disbelief, the relief that coursed through her leaving her weak, exhausted. With a sigh she sank back down on the bed, unable to drag her eyes away from his sleeping face. Gently, with a touch that was feather soft, her fingers skimmed over his cheeks, tracing the tilt of his brows that were somehow arrogant even in sleep, lingering in the thick darkness of hair that brushed his neck. Hot tears stung her eyes. He was all right. He was going to be all right.

For now, a tiny voice in her head reminded her. He was incredibly weak; the fever could come back at any time.

Coldness gripped her, and with a quick silent prayer, her arms slipped around him almost fiercely as she crawled back into bed. *Nothing* was going to happen to him, she vowed. She wouldn't take her eyes off of him for the rest of the night.

* * *

Out of habit and from long years of training, Ross woke abruptly, any traces of sleep vanishing the minute he opened his eyes. Without moving, he lay perfectly still on his back and scanned his surroundings. His gaze was sharp, alert, thorough.

Sunshine streaked through the windowpanes and spilled across the foot of the bed, dancing over the yellow comforter that covered him. There was yellow everywhere—yellow curtains, yellow and white daisies in the short fat vase on the dresser, yellow and white wallpaper...

The wallpaper. He'd recognize it anywhere.

How many miles had he put between West Texas and himself over the past eighteen years? Too many to count, yet his memories had insisted on going with him every step of the way. In a steamy village in South America, he'd watched a small boy help his mother with the family wash... Suddenly Ross found himself back on the ranch, hanging wallpaper for his mother in this very room, laughing with her when he accidently hung one piece upside down.

He was home.

He closed his eyes, savoring the peace that stole through him with unexpected sweetness, savoring the memories that came flooding back with a sigh. Though he hadn't said anything to Sam, there had been times since he'd been shot that he'd wondered if he'd ever see this place again.

How had Sam managed it?

His gaze fell to the woman lying in his arms. She lay on his good side, her arms wrapped around him even in sleep, her breath a warm caress against his shoulder. He smiled at the freckles that dusted her cheeks and pert nose. Then his eyes slid to the sensuous curve of her mouth, lingering. Heat curled into his loins, and unconsciously his arms tightened around her. So much woman in such a little package. How had he made it without her all these years?

He hadn't realized how much he'd needed her. Women were excess baggage, a weakness that he hadn't allowed himself to succumb to. He'd wanted no strings, no clinging vines, no emotional involvements. Because when the next job came along he would leave without a backward glance.

There were no more jobs, though, no more shabby back rooms in the shadows. And Samantha Spencer was no clinging vine. He'd put his life in her hands without a qualm.

His fingers slipped into the wild auburn splendor of her hair as it curled around their entwined bodies. So soft and silky, like her skin, and so reflective of her fighting spirit. He grinned suddenly, remembering her flashing eyes when she'd threatened Raúl with the kerosene lamp. She'd stand toe to toe with the devil himself and spit in his eye.

How had he ever thought she was like the other women who had crossed his path over the years?

Samantha stirred under the fingers that threaded through her hair. The fog of sleep that shrouded her consciousness was thick and warm. She stretched languidly like a waking kitten, her eyes refusing to open and face the sunlight that heated her face. It felt so good just to lie there, her bare legs sliding along Ross's hair-roughened ones.

"Wake up, sleepyhead."

His husky command stroked her like the rough caress of a cat's tongue, pulling her into wakefulness. She moved against him, smiling, loving his closeness. "Mmm. You feel good," she murmured sleepily. "What time is it?"

He glanced at the clock on the nightstand. "Three-fifteen. You'll have to tell me what day it is," he admitted wryly. "I seem to have lost track."

"Lost track?" she repeated dumbly, her mind still fuzzy. She frowned, and suddenly the events of the night came flooding back. Her eyes flew open. "Ross?"

He was waiting for her, his smile crooked. "I'm still with you, Red."

He was conscious. His eyes clear, bright, *smiling*. Her fingers touched his mouth in wonder. "You're all right," she whispered, and burst into tears.

"Honey, don't cry," he exclaimed in surprise as he folded his arms around her tenderly and drew her to him. "Shh, it's okay," he murmured when she buried her face against his neck and all the fears of the past forty-eight hours came pouring out. Her tears always caught him off guard. She was so strong, so tough, yet so utterly defenseless at times. He tended to forget just how delicate she really was.

She cried her heart out, clinging to him, and helplessly Ross tried to comfort her. His hands patted her shaking shoulders, soothing her, sliding over her back, her hips, tangling in her hair, gentling her.

"Aw, love," he whispered, pulling back slightly to kiss her tear-dampened cheeks, "don't cry. I can take anything but that."

His mouth moved to her brow, her wet lashes, her trembling lips. They were so soft, so sweet, so hot. With slow deliberation, he traced the delicate lines of her mouth with his tongue, nibbling, teasing, savoring, silently urging her to forget the strain of the past few days and think of nothing but him. His taste. His scent.

Her sigh was as sweet as honey against his lips. He felt his body tighten with the need to take all of her. Suddenly it was a struggle to keep his mouth light and to show only a trace of the passion that now pushed at him.

Samantha floated under his touch. Her tears dried as her breath quickened; her heart beat crazily until its pounding thundered in her ears. She stirred against him, her body pliant, her lips parting, seeking his, and all Ross's resolves to distract her were lost in the taste of her. With a low growl of approval, he finally took her mouth completely.

Tenderness turned to passion in an instant. This was what she sought, what she needed—his hands heating her skin, trailing fire in their wake as they moved over her, sliding under the football jersey to explore the silken softness of her thighs, the curve of her waist, the fullness of her breasts. She moaned against his mouth, straining against him, the heat that smoldered deep in the center of her flaring into flames of need.

His body was hard and demanding; passion whipped at him. He rolled her to her back in one smooth motion and trapped her beneath him, his hand quickly pushing up the jersey. He wanted to taste every inch of her. "You're beautiful," he rasped, his thumb flicking at the rosy crest of her breast. With a helpless moan, he lowered his head and took her into his mouth.

Samantha gasped, her hands reaching for him, the needs that slammed into her destroying thought. Had she always wanted him this much? Needed him this much? His mouth and teeth tugged a sigh from her. Yes, her heart cried. It seemed as if she'd wanted him forever.

He heard his name on her lips and wondered if she knew how easily she destroyed his control. His body cried out with a need that was hot, throbbing and suddenly draining. With a groan, his mouth returned to hers as he fought the unexpected tiredness that pulled at him.

His kiss was fierce, desperate, and then her mouth was suddenly free, his forehead resting against hers, his breathing labored. Samantha lifted heavy lids and found him staring at her in frustration.

His smile was a wry grimace. "Sorry, sweetheart, but I'm as weak as a kitten!"

Her eyes widened with surprise before gentle laughter tumbled into the sapphire depths. He sounded so disgusted with himself! Didn't he know that all she cared about was that he was alive? "You crazy man," she chided, grinning as she pushed him to his back and leaned over to give him a quick kiss. "I love you."

How easily she said the words. He closed his eyes on a sigh of relief and drew her back to him, his hands buried in her hair. "I thought I'd dreamed that," he admitted thickly.

"No," she said softly, unperturbed that he hadn't repeated the words. He was a cautious man, and the relief she'd heard in his words told her everything her heart needed to hear. She gave him a gentle, soul-destroying kiss, and when she finally lifted her head, tears sparkled freely in her eyes. "I think I loved you from the beginning."

He groaned, tenderness softening the hard lines of his face as he wiped the tears from her cheeks. "There you go again. I suppose you're crying because you're happy?"

"Happy doesn't even touch how I feel. How about you?"

"I'm happy, too," he replied with a wide grin.

"No," she said with a laugh. "How do you *feel*? Are you in pain?"

His gray eyes twinkled devilishly, lingering on where the football jersey rode her hips. "Yeah, but it's not in my shoulder." His grin broadened when she hastily pulled the jersey down. "Where did you get that?"

"It was your brother's."

"I'm sure it looks much better on you than it does on him."

"I think you're right," a masculine voice said dryly.

Their startled eyes flew to the doorway, where Adam stood in jeans and a white shirt, his black cowboy hat pushed to the back of his head, laughter tugging at his mouth. With a gasp, Samantha dove for the robe at the end of the bed and hastily shrugged into it.

Ross stared at the handsome man he knew was his brother and tried to find the eight-year-old boy he had left behind so many years ago. He was there, grinning out of his brown eyes. Ross held out his hand to him. "Baby brother, it's been a long time."

"Yeah," Adam said, chuckling, crossing to take his hand in a firm grip. "When you left, I really was little."

Ross laughed. "Little? Even at eight you were eating us out of house and home. I had to leave just to get a decent meal." Suddenly, with unexpected strength, he tugged on the hand he held and pulled his brother down to give him a fierce hug. "I missed you."

Samantha blinked back tears at the sight of Adam's arms closing around Ross. It was going to be all right. Everything was going to be all right. "I . . . I think I'll go down to the kitchen and fix some soup," she said huskily. They needed some time together to struggle with the awkwardness the passing of time had wrought in their relationship.

Adam's brown eyes were suspiciously bright when he pulled free of Ross's hug and settled into the overstuffed chair next to the bed. He watched Ross's hand grip Samantha, stopping her before she could slide to the side of the bed. "I came up at six to take over my shift," he told them with a wicked grin. "I didn't expect to find Sam in bed with the patient."

"You'd better get used to it," Ross growled huskily.

He nodded, his brown eyes dancing. "Yeah. I saw you were sleeping peacefully, so I figured she was the only medicine you needed."

"If you two are through discussing me," Sam said coolly, cursing the hot color that clung to her fair cheeks, "I'll go fix that soup. Ross is bound to be hungry."

His glowing eyes told her just what he was hungry for, but he only pulled her fingers to his lips for a swift kiss before he released her. "Don't be gone long," he told her softly. "We've still got some unfinished business."

Chapter Twelve

The words "unfinished business" tumbled around in her head, pulling a smile of anticipation from Samantha as she hurried into the bathroom to change into jeans and a white cotton blouse. She struggled for composure, but she couldn't seem to stop grinning. She braided her hair into a thick rope and tossed it over her shoulder to hang down her back, her blue eyes sparkling like sapphires as she studied her appearance in the mirror. The tousled look of sleep was gone; the haunted eyes that had greeted her every time she'd recently looked in the mirror were now bright, clear, and shining with a love she had no need to hide.

Ross loved her. She didn't need the words; his eyes had told her in a hundred ways that words couldn't begin to touch. She'd seen passion there, need, a warmth that went deeper than desire. This was a love that was as unexpected for him as it was for her, like a rose in the desert. She smiled softly. It was all the sweeter for its rareness.

And they had "unfinished business." What promises those words held!

When she returned to his room laden with a tray of steaming vegetable beef soup and crackers, however, her thoughts were on anything but their unfinished business. John and Ginny followed at her heels, John's face grim as he prepared to face his eldest son.

Ross was propped up against the pillows when they walked in, laughing at the tale Adam was telling him about the last roundup. The laughter froze on his face at the sight of his father standing in the doorway.

Time fell away with the blink of an eye, and suddenly it was yesterday. Ross's fingers curled into the sheets, his cool eyes wary, as words that should have never been said echoed in his head. He watched his father's unrelenting features harden into granite and felt something inside himself turn to ice. Eighteen years and nothing had changed. With a silent curse he pushed away the pain and lifted his chin. "Dad," he greeted him stiffly.

John nodded, his expression just as stiff and unyielding as his son's. "How's the shoulder?"

"Sore, but a hell of a lot better than it was."

"Good. Glad to hear it."

Silence fell over the room, threatening to stretch into an eternity. Samantha set the tray on the nightstand, her mouth tight with frustration as her eyes swung to Ross, then his father. How could they be so stubborn? Only last night John had worried that he'd never get the chance to tell Ross how wrong he had been. And now they were acting like strangers!

"Ross..." The words died on her lips at the glittering look he shot her, silently ordering her to stay out of this. But she couldn't. There was too much at stake. "Your father's been worried sick about you," she said pointedly. "We all have."

"I'm fine now," he replied coolly. "I'll be out of here in no time."

"Out of here," Adam repeated in confusion. "But it wasn't ten minutes ago you said—"

"I changed my mind," Ross growled, cutting him off. "I was stupid to think I could come back. You can't ever go back."

Ginny stepped to John Larson's side, her hand at his arm, her green eyes steady as she prompted him toward the bed. "John?"

Why, he's afraid! Samantha realized in surprise as she watched his eyes swing back to his son's bitter face. He's afraid Ross is going to throw his apology back in his face. Did he know his son so little?

He hesitated, pride struggling with the certainty that if he let Ross leave now, he'd never see him again. Without even realizing it, he stepped toward the bed and stopped. "No," he said suddenly, his gray eyes meeting his son's. "You can't go back. But you can start over."

"Where?" Ross demanded suspiciously. "In another state? Another country? Anywhere as long as it's out of your sight?"

That hurt. Samantha flinched at the pain that clouded the older man's face and was mirrored in Ross's. She wanted to stop Ross, to plead with the two of them just to let go, but she knew they couldn't. The past had to be resolved here, now, or it would always be there between them.

"I had that coming," John said tightly. "I...I was wrong, son. For the past eighteen years, there hasn't been a day that I haven't regretted what I said to you when you left."

Eighteen years. Ross stared at the older man, noting the lines that etched his father's face, the gray in the dark hair, the tiredness that clouded his eyes. Those hadn't been there when he'd last seen him.

The loss, the senseless waste of all those years suddenly hit Ross like a fist to the stomach. He could have come home—there had been times when he'd been only hours away—but his pride had always stopped him from being the one to give in. Had it been worth it?

No. The years had been marked with a bitterness that never seemed to go away, a loneliness that stalked him like his shadow. He wanted that forever behind him now.

"I regretted it, too, Dad," he admitted quietly. "I was young and hotheaded, and I guess we both said things we didn't mean." A hesitant smile flickered in his eyes as he stretched out his hand. "I'll forgive you if you'll forgive me."

"That...that sounds reasonable," John said thickly, his eyes suspiciously bright. He clasped Ross's hand as if he could never let it go.

"Hey," Adam teased at the sight of Sam's and Ginny's misty eyes. "Why the tears? This is cause for major celebration! We've got eighteen years to make up for."

"We don't have to do it all today," his father replied with mock sternness. "Ross needs his rest."

"I've also got to talk to Mac," Ross said grimly. "The sooner I give him the information I've got, the sooner he can start closing in on *Los Chisos.*"

"All right," Adam agreed reluctantly. "But just answer one question for now. How did you kidnap Sam?"

Ross laughed and grabbed Samantha's hand, pulling her down to the bed beside him. His eyes danced wickedly as they met hers. "I knocked her out," he replied baldly.

"You what?" John Larson exclaimed.

"Well, Dad, I had to," he defended himself. "I thought she recognized me as an agent, and I was afraid she was going to blow my cover." He turned curious eyes on Samantha. "How *did* you know who I was, Red? I know we'd never met before—I'd have remembered you."

She grinned. "I recognized you as a smuggler named Ross de la Garza. Mac had circulated your picture around the office, along with Raúl's and Manuel's, as part of the ring." She gave a playful tug of his beard. "With this and the long hair, you looked just as scrungy as they did. I would never have guessed you weren't one of them."

He chuckled. "Thanks—I think." His hand slipped under her hair to cup the back of her neck and tug her close for a kiss. He meant to keep it light, quick, teasing, but at the taste of her, he forgot the eyes watching them; he forgot everything but the sweetness of her mouth.

Samantha's fingers fluttered up to rest on his chest, a mute appeal against the overwhelming need to melt against him and lose herself in him. Dear God, how could he turn her bones to putty with just a kiss?

"Ross." The words were murmured against his lips before she reluctantly dragged her mouth free. "I...need to call Mac," she finally managed huskily. "He wanted to talk to you as soon as you were better."

"I'll call him," Ginny volunteered as she saw Samantha start to rise from the side of the bed. "I've got to be going, and I'll make the call on my way out."

"But aren't you staying for a while?" Samantha asked in surprise, frowning as the older woman suddenly bustled about as if she had to rush off to keep an appointment. "Since Ross is better, we can relax and—"

Ginny shook her curly white head firmly. "No, dear. The family needs some time without outsiders."

"You're hardly an outsider, Ginny," John Larson told her quietly, immediately drawing her eyes to him. "Why don't you stay?"

Puzzled, Samantha watched a silent message pass between the two of them. Ginny seemed agitated, torn between the need to stay and the urge to leave, but finally she shook her head, her softly rounded chin set determinedly. "I don't think so," she said softly.

"You and Ross have a lot to catch up on. You don't need me."

Samantha wanted to protest, but when John said nothing else to dissuade the older woman, the words died in her throat. Instead she said, "Thank you for everything Ginny. I don't know what we would have done without you."

"It was nothing, dear. I'm just glad Ross is better." She hurried to the door, only to stop on the threshold. "Would you like for me to call Mac and have him come out to the ranch?"

Helplessly Samantha sat back down next to Ross. "If you don't mind... I left his number on a pad next to the telephone. He's anxious to talk to Ross, so he'll probably rush right out here."

"I'll let you know if there's a problem," she promised and quickly hurried downstairs. The words were hardly out of her mouth before Ginny nodded.

John Larson shook his head, his expression somber as he sank heavily into the ladder-backed chair that sat next to the door. "Sometimes I'd like to throttle that woman," he said in the empty silence that followed Ginny's leave-taking. "I've been trying to get her to marry me for years."

Samantha stared at him in surprise. "You have?"

The older man's smile was slow, rueful. "I've asked her every year for the past ten years, and every year the answer's been the same. No."

Ten years? Unconsciously Samantha's eyes shifted to Ross. He hadn't said a word. He'd been close to his mother, devastated by her death. After all this time, would he resent his father loving another woman?

"It's obvious she loves you," Ross stated quietly. At Samantha's anxious look, he smiled and squeezed her hand reassuringly. "Why won't she marry you?"

"She's afraid," his father answered flatly. "She's afraid you boys will resent her, that what we have is just friendship, that after all these years she might be making a mistake. She lost her first husband at the age of nineteen, and she hardly remembers what it was like to be married."

"Surely there must be a way for you to convince her," Ross said with a frown. "You've both been alone too long."

"Ginny can be as stubborn as a mule. She won't be pushed."

"I've been trying to give him tips on handling women," Adam said teasingly, deliberately lightening the mood. "But he just won't listen."

Ross grinned broadly. "And when did you get to be such a Casanova?"

"Hey, the women just drop at my feet," he replied innocently. "Can I help it if they find me attractive?"

Samantha's lips twitched. "I think I'm going to be sick," she said dryly.

"Is he always this obnoxious?" Ross laughingly demanded of his father.

"No, sometimes he's worse."

Adam's eyes twinkled at the sound of their groans. "You're just jealous because I'm a legend."

"In your own mind," Ross retorted, collapsing back against the pillow with a chuckle. His hand went to the bandage at his shoulder, his dark brows knitting in irritation as the ache of discomfort became a throb.

Samantha noted the unconscious gesture with a frown of concern. "You should rest now," she told him quietly.

"That's right," Adam said promptly, jumping to his feet to head for the door. "Tonight we'll celebrate. I'll go check the kitchen and see if we've got any champagne."

John Larson rose, too. "Sam's right. We'll have plenty of time to talk when you're feeling stronger."

"Dad, wait." Ross's call stopped him at the door. He motioned to the overstuffed chair near the bed. "Sit a minute." His fingers tightened around Samantha's as she started to move off the bed. At her look of surprise, he said, "No, stay. I want you to hear this, too."

His eyes traveled around the room, noting both the changes that had taken place since he'd left, and the traces of the past that still lingered. He sighed and met his father's eyes. "I'm home for good. I've been wanting to come back for a long time, but the government kept dangling jobs in front of me with the promise that the next one would be the last. This time I'm holding them to it."

The relief that coursed through John Larson was carefully hidden behind a frown of concern. "Are you sure, son? Things haven't changed around here that much since you left. You know it can be damn dull at times."

"Dad, I've had enough excitement over the past eighteen years to last me a lifetime," he said with a laugh. "I promised myself a long time ago if I ever stepped foot in Texas again, nothing short of a nuclear explosion would make me leave. I'm staying."

Laughter bubbled up in Samantha as his words echoed in her heart. He wasn't leaving! Did he have any idea how long she had been dreading the moment when she would have to watch him walk away from her? Her fingers clutched at his.

Ross felt her surprise, her relief, with a sense of shock. Had she really expected him to leave? To just walk away as if she were just another woman he'd come across on an assignment? She was his! Surely she knew that.

He started to reassure her, then stopped. This wasn't the time. Later, when they were alone, he would show her that she had no reason to doubt him or the future. He squeezed her hand and turned his attention back to his father.

"Dad?" he asked hesitantly at the older man's silence. "I thought you'd be glad to know I've finally decided to settle down."

John Larson struggled with a flood of emotions that threatened to swamp him. Relief, thankfulness, love. After all these years, the family was finally going to be together again. "I am," he replied thickly. "I...Adam and I could use some help around the ranch. If you're interested," he quickly amended. Never again would he make the mistake of trying to decide the future for either one of his sons. "If you've got other plans—"

"I thought you'd never ask," Ross quickly assured him. He laughed suddenly, dispelling the shadowy memory of that long-ago argument. "It's been a long time since I branded a calf. Are you going to trust me with your prize cattle?''

"Yes." His answer was quick and sure. And that quickly, the breach was healed.

Ross closed his eyes on a sigh. "Damn, it's good to be home."

"Rest now," Samantha whispered as she leaned over to give him a tender kiss. "Mac will be here soon and you'll need all your strength for that."

He wanted to argue—he didn't need rest, he just needed her at his side—but his eyes were suddenly heavy, his energy nonexistent. "I don't seem to have any choice in the matter," he grumbled weakly. "I can't keep my damn eyes open."

They left him to his sleep, but within an hour, he was awake and impatient with the forced inactivity. "Sam! Dad! Hey, is anybody home?"

Samantha poked her head around the door and tried to appear disapproving, but at the sight of his thunderous expression, she grinned. "You're supposed to be resting."

His response was short, rude, unprintable. When she only laughed, he threw a pillow at her. "I don't like being an invalid. It's too dull. Come here, witch, and cheer me up."

"Now, now, children, none of that," Adam teased as he stepped around Samantha and came into the room, balancing a takeout box of pizza and a six-pack of beer. "It's party time."

"I thought we were having champagne," Ross retorted with a grin when Adam set the food on the dresser.

"We were out. You can't have any, anyway. You can't mix drugs and alcohol," he reminded him, his brown eyes dancing wickedly. "You're having chicken soup and milk."

"The hell I am!" Ross growled. "Not when you're having pizza and beer. Sam, bring me a piece of that pizza before I have to get out of this bed and take my little brother down a peg or two."

"I don't think I should get involved in a sibling argument," she said innocently, making no attempt to hold back a smile. "On the other hand," she said with a chuckle when his eyes narrowed dangerously, "you need to keep your strength up."

"Aw, come on, Sam," Adam groaned, "don't let him push you around with that cold stare of his. He's been fooling people with that since I was a kid."

"It worked, too, didn't it?" Ross laughed, unrepentant, as Sam handed him a slice of pizza. "I kept you in line."

"And who kept you in line?" his father demanded, his gray eyes twinkling as he suddenly appeared in the doorway. "Just remember that, now that you're going to be working on the ranch again."

"Working on the ranch!" Adam exclaimed, a slice of pizza held halfway to his mouth. "Hey, that's great! You can be in charge of Romeo."

Ross eyed his brother suspiciously. "Romeo?"

"Yeah." Mischief danced in his brown eyes. "He's one of Dad's prize longhorn bulls. For the past three years, he's been a pain in the butt. He goes courting his girlfriends on neighboring ranches, and nothing we've been able to do has kept that animal in."

"But how does he get out?" Samantha asked, laughing.

"He jumps the fence!" he replied in disgust. "There's not a cow within seven counties that's escaped his attention, and I've gotten calls from up to fifty miles away about him. Go ahead and laugh," he told his brother gleefully. "You won't be laughing when someone calls you at three in the morning to come and pick him up."

"I didn't come home to baby-sit a bull with spring fever," Ross said, chuckling. "If you can't control him, how do you expect me to?"

"You're smart, big brother. You'll think of something."

Ross snorted disdainfully, but his lips twitched traitorously, and they all laughed. Samantha sat on the edge of the bed as they devoured the rest of the pizza, and absently Ross's fingers played with her hair. If this assignment hadn't come along, how many more years would have passed before he swallowed his pride and came home? Thank God for Mac and the excuse he gave him to come back.

He frowned, tugging on Sam's hair. "Where the hell is Mac?" he asked her. "He's had plenty of time to get here by now."

She'd been wondering the same thing. "He could have gotten tied up at the station," she said as she came to her feet. "I'll go call him and see if there's a problem."

But she hadn't even reached the door, when a shrill alarm suddenly ripped through the quiet of approaching evening. "What the hell!" John Larson exclaimed, and hurried to the window.

"What is it?" Ross demanded harshly, wincing as he swiveled to watch his father.

"The fire alarm on the windmill," Adam cried as he and Samantha joined the older man at the window. His eyes widened at the sight of the flames licking at a building on a small rise about half a mile from the house. "Dad, that's one of the barns! The horses!"

"Get the truck," his father ordered. "We're going to need every available hand."

Adam sprinted out of the room. "I'm going with you," Ross stated flatly, and swung his feet to the side of the bed. The pain that twisted in his shoulder drained the blood from his face.

Samantha whirled from the window in alarm. "No, you're not!"

"Get back in that bed!" John Larson barked. "What the hell do you think you're doing?"

Ross collapsed against the pillows, his breath coming in gasps. He closed his eyes weakly. "Damn it," he whispered. "You need help and I don't even have the strength to get out of bed!"

Samantha rushed to his side and pulled the covers back up to his chest. "Idiot!" she scolded softly. "You move one more time and I'm going to hog-tie you to this bed."

John's thunderous scowl lifted at the sight of Samantha bending over his son and Ross's hands pulling her close. "Adam will have the truck out front by now, and the volunteer fire department will be here any minute. I'll leave you to keep Ross in bed, Sam."

Samantha's blue eyes sparkled as they locked with Ross's. "Did you hear that?" she teased as the older man rushed out of the room. "Got any ideas how I can keep you in bed?"

"A few," he drawled as he tangled his fingers in her hair and tugged her mouth within inches of his. His grin flashed wickedly. "And if I weren't weak as a kitten right now, I'd show them to you."

"No," she corrected him with a laugh, "you'd be out there fighting that fire with Adam and your father."

"You're right," he agreed. His brows drew together in a scowl as he glared at the window. "I don't like being so helpless!"

"I could go for you..." she began hesitantly.

"No!" His fingers bit into her arms to give her a swift shake. "I'm not letting you out of my sight. I know what a daredevil you are, and you're not going anywhere." Suddenly tender, he released her arms, only to frame her face with his hands. His eyes caressed her. "I want you in one piece when I marry you."

Samantha dragged in a surprised breath, her eyes wide as she searched his face for signs of joking. All she saw was love. "Ross..." She struggled with a sudden rush of tears, her lips trembling as she ran her fingers over the curve of his cheek in wonder. When he caught her hand and pulled it to his mouth for a soft kiss, the foolish tears spilled over. "Are you asking me or telling me to marry you?" she whispered, her smile watery.

The sight of her tears would always be able to destroy him. He wiped them away with fingers that were gentle, cherishing. "That depends," he admitted huskily. "If your answer is yes, I'm asking you. If it's no, then I'm telling you, and you're not getting out of this bed until I can change your mind. So what's it going to be?"

Did he even have to ask? she wondered wildly. Could he really be so unsure of himself and of her love for him? She lifted anxious eyes to his and saw the wariness, the caution. Her heart jerked in surprise. Why hadn't she seen that the years of loneliness had taught him to guard his heart as carefully as he did his life?

She flicked his hair back from his forehead and smiled down into his eyes. "No has interesting possibilities," she said softly, "but since you're *asking*, I'm accepting."

"That's a yes?" he demanded, his gaze intense.

She laughed and melted against his chest, careful not to put any weight against his wound. "Yes!" she said, raining kisses over his face. "Positively, unequivocally, eternally yes! Forever. Is that long enough for you, you foolish man?"

"Not nearly," he growled, pulling her down to him. "But it'll do for starters."

He took her mouth hungrily, sweetly, demanding everything of her, giving her his heart, his soul. His arms trapped her close, urging her closer, until she stretched out on the bed, her sigh soft and moist against his lips, her legs tangled with his. No, an eternity wasn't nearly long enough with this woman, he thought with a groan as her hands swept over him like the wings of a butterfly.

"Are you sure?" he demanded against her mouth. "Be sure, Sam, because once you're mine, I could never let you go." His fingers tightened in her hair. "I'm a possessive man."

Yes, he was. Possessive, arrogant at times, proud, a man used to having his orders obeyed without question. Their life together would not be tame. She grinned. A placid, serene relationship would bore her to tears.

"We'll fight, you know," she teased as she wound her arms around his neck and let her fingers play in his dark hair. "I can be pretty stubborn when I set my mind to it."

"I noticed that," he said thoughtfully, love and laughter warming his eyes as he just barely resisted the urge to crush her to him. Her touch made it almost impossible to think. "But I know how to get around you." He trailed a finger down her neck and over her breast, slowly circling the sensitive peak, watching her eyes darken and smolder with hidden fires. His gaze locked with hers as he grinned wickedly. "See?"

Samantha struggled to find her voice. "That's cheating," she rasped.

"Mmm-hmm. But it feels good, doesn't it?"

It felt heavenly. She closed her eyes and buried her head against the side of his neck. "Two can play at that game," she murmured against his skin. Her hands explored him lazily, sliding from his chest down to the waistband of his jockey shorts. With teasing slowness, her fingers slipped under the elastic. He stiffened, drawing a soft laugh from her. "Winning an argument should be very interesting."

"We can't lose," he groaned as her hands found him. "Sam...honey...you're driving me crazy!"

He felt her smile against his skin. "Good," she whispered. "Lie back and enjoy it."

How could he enjoy madness? he wondered as she pushed him to his back and planted slow, lingering kisses at the corners of his mouth. But he did. Her hands moved over him as if they had all the time in the world, wooing him, seducing him until his limbs were weighted, the throbbing in his loins a sweet ache. And still she tarried, the clean intoxicating scent of her attacking his senses as surely as the delicious flick of her tongue teasing his mouth. With a moan of desperation, his fingers curled into the wild splendor of her hair to hold her still for a scorching kiss.

Samantha's heart quickened, the heat that streaked through her like starlight in her blood, setting her aglow. He loved her, and the future was more than just a dream, a hope. He was hers forever, to touch, to kiss, to love. The knowledge set bells ringing in her ears. She arched against him, lost in the feel of him, the taste of him.

Desire covered him with a silken net, pulling him toward a drugging darkness that was hot, sweet, savage. But on the edge of sanity, bells rang in alarm. He frowned, suddenly remembering. "The bells," he muttered, dragging his mouth free to taste the pulse pounding in her neck. He dragged in a shuddering breath and fought the urge to lose himself in Samantha's pliant body. "The volunteer fire department must have arrived." His fingers moved in her hair, unconsciously savoring its softness. "I hope they got here in time."

Samantha blinked in confusion and slowly came back to earth. She'd forgotten the fire. It was nothing compared to the one that raged in her blood. She sighed and tried to still the pounding of her heart. "Your...father and Adam will have gotten the horses out."

"Go look," he prompted her huskily, kissing her neck one last time before releasing her. "Can you see if it's spread any or just contained to the barn?"

The blaze was like a bonfire in the darkness of early evening. Samantha stared at it, aghast. "Oh, Ross, it's terrible! The whole barn's gone up in flames." Shadowy figures moved about as the volunteers sprang into action, but their efforts were too little, too late. "I can see quite a few horses, so your father and Adam must have gotten there in time, but the barn's a total loss." Her troubled eyes turned back to his. "I'm sorry."

"Damn!" He leaned his head back against the pillows, his face grim. "If I hadn't been laid up with this shoulder, I might have been able to help."

"But you couldn't have put it out," she argued, coming back to his side. "It was already too far gone by the time the alarm went off."

He took her hand, his thumb absently rubbing her knuckles, his smile a grimace. "Yeah, you're right, but I hate lying here not being able to help."

"You've got plenty of time to help. Once your shoulder's healed and this smuggling mess is cleared up, your father will probably work your tail off." Her blue eyes danced teasingly. "You'll be too tired to do anything at night but sleep."

"Don't you believe it," he growled, and pulled her down for a swift hard kiss. When he freed her, he was frowning. "And speaking of smugglers, where the hell is Mac?"

"Mac won't be coming," a familiar voice said from the doorway.

Chapter Thirteen

Samantha gasped, her startled eyes flying to the man who stepped into the bedroom on silent feet. David Martínez. He stood less than two feet from the end of the bed. His black shirt and slacks seemed sinister against the brightness of the room's yellow decor; the small revolver in his hand looked ugly, deadly. And it was trained right at Ross's heart.

Fear trailed icy fingers down her spine, chilling her soul. Unconsciously she clutched at Ross's hand. "David!" she whispered, her gaze riveted to the gun in horror. "What are you doing?"

"What does it look like I'm doing?" he countered, his ugly smile cool and menacing. "I'm tying up a few loose ends." His black eyes slid to the man at her side. "Ah, the prodigal son. Ross de la Garza. Who would have ever suspected that under that mangy, long-haired exterior was a Larson? And a government agent?" His smile became evil as he watched Ross stiffen. "Make one move, Larson, and it'll be your last. This time I won't miss your heart."

Only a fool would have doubted David's sincerity. Slowly, deliberately, Ross forced himself to relax against the pillows at his back. His eyes narrowed to mere slits, he gave Sam's hand an imperceptible squeeze as every muscle in his body tensed for action. The wheels in his head clicked furiously.

"This time?" he asked David archly. "I was under the impression that L.J. was responsible for that. Are the two of you working together?"

"L.J.'s dead," Samantha told Ross hollowly before the other man could answer. "David and L.J. volunteered to rescue me, but when L.J. shot you, David had to kill him—" The words died on her lips as the pieces suddenly came together. Stricken, she stared at David. "It wasn't L.J.," she choked, shrinking against Ross. "It was you! You were the one trying to kill us, and L.J. saw you! That's why you killed him. He witnessed the whole thing."

"He left me no choice," David replied indifferently. "Once you let it slip that Ross was working undercover, I knew I had to get rid of both of you. L.J. was in the way."

In the way? she silently screamed in growing terror. He was in the way, so David just cold-bloodedly shot him down! Then he returned to the station with a bald-faced lie that conveniently shifted the blame to L.J. How could they have been so blind?

"You planned to kill me all along," she said flatly. "That's why you insisted on coming with L.J."

"No." For just a moment, the ruthless lines of his face softened, and he was once again the man she had worked with and trusted for the past two months. "I really did intend to bring you back," he told her quietly. "You didn't know anything that could hurt me. Oh, you could identify Raúl and Manuel, but Mac already knew they were involved. I didn't trust them to let you go, so I came after you." He glared at Ross, his dark eyes glittering with cold anger. "If it hadn't been for you, I would have been able to return her unharmed to Mac."

"And received all the glory for rescuing her," Ross sneered. "Very commendable."

David's expression turned glacial. "You should have died in Mexico. You would have saved me a lot of trouble."

"Sorry to disappoint you," Ross taunted, "but I have no intention of dying just to suit you."

This couldn't be happening! Samantha sat as if turned to stone, her mouth dry, the taste of terror bitter on her tongue. Her heart hammered in her chest, echoing loudly in her ears, until she was achingly aware of the awful, empty silence of the house. They were alone, unarmed, at David's mercy. But he had none. From the corner of her eye, she looked toward the window and saw the darkness that had fallen since Adam and John had left. How long had they been gone? How long would it be before they returned? Time. They needed time.

"D-David." She winced at the unsteadiness of her voice and struggled for control. When she finally spoke, it was with a calmness she was far from feeling. "You'll never get away with this. Can't you see that? Mac isn't an idiot. You've fooled him for now, but he'll figure out that L.J. wasn't the informant, and then he'll come looking for you. He won't rest until he catches you."

"He won't catch me," he replied smuggly. "The old fool wouldn't even know where to look."

Samantha's eyes flashed. "Be careful who you call a fool. From where I'm standing, that shoe fits you. *You* are the one who's taking the risk for *El Chiso*. You're doing all the dirty work, taking all the chances, and who's getting all the money?" she taunted. "*El Chiso*, that's who!"

David's mocking laughter slid down her spine like a snake. "You just don't get it, do you, Sam?" he jeered. "I am *El Chiso*."

The blood drained from her face. "No!" she whispered, stunned. He couldn't be! How could she have worked alongside him and never seen, never even suspected the cruelty he was capable of? "Oh, God, how could you?"

"You son of a bitch," Ross purred. His eyes were hard as they swept over the man whose footsteps he'd been dogging for two solid months. He was well built, with broad shoulders and slim hips, his swarthy, good-looking face just a little too soft. Scum, Ross decided. He was worse than scum, with a soul as black as his clothes.

And the odds were all on his side.

Ross cursed silently, not liking the cold air of calm that the other man wore like a suit of armor. If he was nervous, fidgety, there would be room for a distraction. But David's cool determination made no allowances for doubts, for emotions. He'd kill them both and never bat an eye.

With a quiet, furious oath, Ross wished in vain for a weapon, his fingers tight around Sam's.

Sam. He'd give anything to have her a thousand miles away from here. Safe, he wanted her safe, not at the mercy of a coldhearted fiend while he lay helpless in bed.

He was not going to let him kill her.

The thought came to Ross coolly, rationally, turning the fire that raged in his blood to ice. And he welcomed the ice like a long-lost friend. For eighteen years, he'd walked on the edge of danger by remaining detached, freezing his emotions. David Martínez was no different from any of the other unprincipled thieves he'd come up against in the past. Somehow he was going to take him apart, piece by piece, and enjoy every minute of it.

The images that sprang to mind brought a brittle, cold light to Ross's eyes. "You think you're real clever, don't you?" he taunted. "A border patrol agent and head of the biggest smuggling ring in West Texas. No one would ever suspect."

"It was the perfect cover," the other man admitted, a self-satisfied smile playing about his mouth. "I knew everything that was going on on both sides of the law. But things slipped up when Sam talked Mac into letting her stake out that section of the river."

Resentment hardened his lips into a thin line. "You should have stayed away from there, Sam. None of this would ever have happened if you'd have done as you were told. But, no, you had to argue with Mac and get him to change the assignments after it was too late for me to contact Manuel. If you'd just stayed away..."

"L.J. would still be alive," she said tightly, forcing herself to say the words. "But you'd have been no better off than you are today. The day you smuggled your first alien across the river you set yourself up to get caught. It was just a matter of time." Her eyes locked with his. "Why'd you do it, David? Why?"

A dark brow lifted arrogantly. "Isn't it obvious? You know how bad the conditions are in Mexico. If oil prices keep going down, they'll get even worse. My people are there. I had to help them—"

Samantha cursed softly, cutting him off cold. "I hadn't realized you were such a philanthropist," she sneered. "Do you honestly expect us to believe that crap? If you wanted to *help* your people, you wouldn't charge them their life savings to bring them across the river, then rob and abandon them." Her blue eyes raked him contemptuously. "Admit it, David. You were doing it for the money. You couldn't care less about *your people*."

He shrugged, unconcerned. "Only a fool would turn his back on that kind of money."

"And only a fool would expect to get away with murdering two U.S. government agents," Ross told him silkily. "It won't matter where you run, what hole you slide into, Mac will track you down and bring you to justice." He smiled wickedly. "Think about it, Martínez. For the rest of your life, you'll be looking over your shoulder, always watching the shadows, waiting to get caught. You won't even be able to close your eyes at night without wondering if someone will slip up on you in the dark."

David laughed softly, mockingly. "Nice try, but there's only one problem with your scenario. No one will even suspect me of killing you. You see, I went in this afternoon and handed in my resignation. Mac was really sorry to hear that my father had suffered a stroke and I had to return to the family ranch outside of Mexico City."

He stepped closer to the bed, the gun pointed unwaveringly at Ross, genuine amusement lighting his face. "He's really short-handed right now with L.J. dead and Sam out of commission. He was so snowed under, I took some of his calls while I was cleaning out my desk. One of them was from a Ginny Nelson."

Mac never got Ginny's call that Ross was ready to talk to him. The thought hit Samantha like a blow to the stomach. They'd all been too exhausted to realize Ginny would never recognize Mac's voice, or that her offer to make the call could result in danger to Ross. Mac wasn't coming.

"So you see," David continued with a malicious grin, "there's no help coming, no witnesses to pin this on me. Everyone at the station thinks I left this afternoon. By the time the fire is put out, you'll be dead and I'll be safely across the river, never to be seen again. Mac will naturally assume that Raúl and Manuel finally tracked you down."

Samantha stared at him in horror. "You started the fire."

Her outrage only broadened his grin. "You should know by now I never leave anything to chance. I knew Ross wouldn't be able to help with the fire and that you would probably be at his side. Right where I wanted you."

"Someone will be after you within the hour," Ross promised him softly. "You kill us with a government-issued gun, and you're signing your own death warrant."

The amusement on the other man's face never even flickered at the gibe. "Surely you don't think I'm that stupid." He showed Ross the gun. "Recognize it? It's one of your father's. You know, he really should lock his gun cabinet. You never know when someone's going to walk in, help himself to a pistol and kill the family in their beds. Tragic, isn't it?"

He was mad, Samantha thought wildly, drunk on his own cunning. At her side, she felt the barely leashed tension in Ross. Her heart skidded in alarm. He wouldn't patiently lie there and wait to die. "David, please," she begged, hating to plead, but knowing she would go down on her knees to save Ross, "don't do this! Think what you're doing, what you're throwing away—"

"Samantha? Ross?"

Samantha gasped, horrified, as Ginny's breathless voice floated ahead of her into the guest room as she trudged up the stairs. A cry of warning trembled on Samantha's lips, but David turned the gun on her, and the words strangled in her throat.

"I saw the fire from my house and got over here as fast as I could," Ginny explained as she approached the bedroom. "John suggested I make some iced tea and sandwiches for the men. They'll be hungry—"

She stopped in the doorway, winded, her white hair disheveled, her rounded cheeks flushed from the climb and the soft rouge she invariably wore. Her quick eyes summed up the situation in an instant, her sudden paleness the only sign of her distress. Her sharp gaze rested on Samantha and Ross. "Are you two all right?" she asked quietly, ignoring David and the gun he still pointed at Ross.

"Get over by the bed," David ordered sharply, motioning with the gun. He shifted his position so that with only the slightest movement of his hand, he could shoot any one of them. "This was not a good time for you to be neighborly," he told Ginny coldly. "Not a good time at all. You've complicated things, Mrs. Nelson, and I don't like complications."

Ginny stood straight and uncowering at Samantha's side. She recognized him, of course. As a border agent, he had access to all the local ranches; at one time or another he'd dealt with all the ranchers, including Ginny. "I'm not especially fond of them myself, Mr. Martínez. Don't complicate matters further by pulling that trigger."

"Ah, but I have to," he insisted with a cold smile. "Ross and Samantha know too much. And you're a witness I can't afford." His eyes slid to Ross. "You first, Larson, for all the hell you've caused me."

Ross heard Samantha and Ginny gasp in horror, but his eyes were glued to David's. The cold, passionless calm that had settled over him was as familiar as the adrenaline that always pumped through his veins at the stench of danger. He'd have a split second, maybe less, to jump out of the way of certain death. His only hope was to watch David's eyes. His eyes would give him away.

Samantha watched David's finger tighten on the trigger, black terror welling in her, choking her. Ross! Oh, God, David was going to shoot him again, and this time he'd put a bullet straight through his heart.

The silence in the room seemed to stretch into an eternity. Then suddenly, almost imperceptibly, the merciless lines of David's face became deadly.

"No!" Samantha screamed, and launched herself across the bed at David at the exact moment a shot was fired. "Oh, God, no!"

She slammed into him, knocking the gun to the floor, but it was too late. Tears streamed down her face. "You bastard!" she cried, pounding him with her fists, staggering him, in her hurt blind to everything but the need to strike out at him. "How could you? *How could you!"*

"Sam? Sam, honey?" Ross called sharply, pushing himself up from the floor where he had rolled at the same moment Sam had thrown herself at David. "I'm all right. Quit crying and look at me."

"Ross?" She whirled, her eyes desperate and dark with pain, and found him pulling himself up on the bed. He grinned crookedly. "But . . . how . . ."

Stunned, her gaze shifted to David. He leaned weakly against the wall, his hand pressed to his shoulder, blood oozing between his fingers. "David, you've been shot," she said numbly.

"It's all right, Sam," John Larson assured her quietly from the doorway. "You're safe now."

His face was grimy with soot and sweat, his jaw set in that strong determined way that was so like Ross's, his gray eyes as cold as a blue norther as they rested on David. In his hand was a black revolver.

Samantha stared at the gun, mesmerized. The shadows that clouded her eye grew dark, crowding her mind. Ross was safe; they were all safe. She frowned, trying to take it all in, but the blackness was all-encompassing, closing out John, the gun, Ross. Without a murmur of protest, she slid into the void; and for the first time in her life she fainted.

Epilogue

A fire crackled in the rough stone fireplace, the golden, licking flames the only source of light in the dark bedroom. It was a cold night, quiet but for the hiss of the fire and the soft laughter and sighs that came from the shadowed recesses of the bed.

Under the old-fashioned quilt, Samantha curled up against Ross, unmindful of the room's chilliness as long as she was in his arms. She flicked at a male nipple with her tongue, laughing softly when he growled in pleasure. "This hunting cabin is a perfect place for a honeymoon," she said as she pulled back to smile up at him. Her fingers marveled at the rock-hard smoothness of his freshly shaved jaw before moving to his nape, brushing at the now neat, conservative cut of his dark hair. "Do you think your father and Ginny will use it now that she's finally agreed to marry him?"

"I don't know. Dad mentioned turning a cattle-buying trip to Argentina into an extended honeymoon." He laughed softly. "I think he's still in shock that she said yes."

"She finally realized that she could lose him just as easily as he nearly lost her. She wanted the rest of her life with him instead of just scattered moments." Samantha's searching fingers moved to his ear. "Remind me to thank your father for thinking of the cabin."

He grabbed her hand and drew it to his mouth, planting a scorching kiss on the inside of her wrist. When her pulse thundered against his lips, he grinned wickedly. "After everything that happened, he was afraid you'd have nothing but bad memories of the ranch. He hoped this would make up for it."

"Oh, *this* makes up for everything," she murmured huskily, rubbing her bare foot up and down his hair-roughened calf. "Were we only married this morning? You make me forget the world."

"That's only fair. You've been driving me crazy ever since I met you," he admitted thickly, nuzzling her neck before sliding his mouth up the side of her neck to nibble at her ear. At her soft moan, his knee nudged her legs apart, the hunger that he had thought slaked only moments before suddenly smoldering. His hands played over her, seeking her softness, her heat. "I couldn't even do my job without thinking of you, wanting you."

"Oh, Ross!" Her arms locked around him fiercely. "I was so afraid I was going to lose you. David—"

"David's safely behind bars, love," he reassured her, holding her close. "And Raúl and Manuel were picked up trying to follow our tracks across the river." Flashes of that night two weeks ago flickered in his head, turning his face grim. He'd never felt so helpless as when he'd lain in bed and waited for death, knowing that Sam would be next. "They'll never terrorize the border again. And thanks to Dad, David now knows what it feels like to be shot in the shoulder."

"I couldn't believe it when I turned and saw John standing in the doorway with that gun."

"What a baby!" Ross teased, grinning mischievously. "Fainting when it was all over with. You'd been kidnapped, dragged through the desert, threatened with rape and shot at. But the minute you're safe, you faint dead away. If that's not just like a—"

"Don't you dare say 'woman,'" Samantha warned him, her blue eyes sparkling. "I wasn't the one lying in bed too weak to do anything," she reminded him impishly. "And I'm not talking about stopping David from killing us."

"I thought I made up for that," he growled, and rolled her to her back, taking her mouth in a fierce, possessive kiss. Would he ever get enough of her? he wondered, groaning as the heat in his loins streaked through him. She had only to smile and he wanted her, only to let him touch her and he wanted to taste her, savor every sweet, smooth, silken inch of her. When he kissed her, the soft sounds she made in the back of her throat pulled him into mindlessness. And now she was his. Forever.

Samantha's hands danced over him, the ache that burned deep inside her pushing aside everything but the need to be one with the man she loved. Her mouth charted the angles and planes of his face, discovering as if for the first time the feel of him under her lips.

He was everything she'd always wanted, all she'd ever need. Without his having asked her, she'd handed in her resignation to Mac. She hadn't wanted anything to come between Ross and her, especially fear for her safety. Ironically, she'd discovered that what her family had always wanted for her was what she really wanted, too. Her search for excitement was over. She'd found it in the man at her side.

But one fear still nagged at her. "No regrets about giving up your job to return to the ranch?" she whispered near his ear, voicing it for the first time. "I don't want you to miss the excitement. I know how addictive it can be."

His hands tangled in her hair, capturing her face between his palms so his eyes could meet hers in the shadowed light. "There are different kinds of excitement," he told her in a low, rough voice. "I've grown tired of the kind I found working for the government. I don't need it now." His thumbs gently rubbed her cheeks. "I need you. *I love you*. My life will never be dull as long as I have your love."

Tears sparkled in her eyes. She had given him her body, her love, her heart. Together they would have